Covert Joy

ALSO BY CLARICE LISPECTOR

AVAILABLE FROM NEW DIRECTIONS

COVERT JOY
selected stories

Clarice Lispector

Translation and afterword by Katrina Dodson

Introduction by Rachel Kushner

Edited by Benjamin Moser

A NEW DIRECTIONS BOOK

Published in cloth by New Directions in 2025
Manufactured in the United States of America

Library of Congress Cataloging-in-Publication Data
Names: Lispector, Clarice, author. | Dodson, Katrina, translator, writer of after-
word. | Kushner, Rachel, writer of introduction. | Moser, Benjamin, editor.
Title: Covert joy : selected stories / Clarice Lispector ; translation and afterword
by Katrina Dodson ; introduction by Rachel Kushner ; edited by Benjamin Moser.
Other titles: Covert joy (Compilation)
Description: First edition. | New York : New Directions Publishing, 2025.
Identifiers: LCCN 2024048698 | ISBN 9780811238878 (paperback)
Subjects: LCSH: Lispector, Clarice—Translations into English. | LCGFT: Short
stories.
Classification: LCC PQ9697.L585 C69 2025 | DDC 869.3/42—dc23/eng/20241108
LC record available at https://lccn.loc.gov/2024048698

10 9 8 7 6 5 4 3 2 1

New Directions Books are published for James Laughlin
by New Directions Publishing Corporation
80 Eighth Avenue, New York 10011

Contents

A Gram of Radium

I'M TEMPTED TO SUGGEST YOU SKIP THIS INTRODUC-
tion and save your energy for Clarice Lispector, but she will
give you energy instead of taking yours away. The fruits of
her project—both an art and a philosophy (ontological, but
also chosen, deliberate, *developed*)—are strangely restorative.
While reading itself is not passive, you can relax, while she is
hard at work, asking questions that are inside you, too, so that
you yourself don't have to frame them. Her aspiration is nothing less than to uncover the bizarre mystery of consciousness,
to contemplate being while being, to apprehend life while living it. Someone has to do this work. Lispector seems to have
recognized that she had a gift for the job and plunged in. I'm
not claiming she made art as self-sacrifice. But in some eternal
space, the philosophical boiler room of the world, the secret
alcove behind a heavy velvet drape, she is yet tarrying in the
void, the same void that in you and me is repressed for the sake
of appearances. For the sake of "reality."

The twenty short stories collected here are a perfect gather-
ing of Lispectarian types: of people, epiphany, mystery. If her
grand oeuvre of short fictions forms a kind of pastiche painting,

here you can see, spotlit, key scenes: A housewife encounters a blind man on a tram and is destabilized by her own benevolence. A chicken is granted clemency after laying an egg, but cannot comprehend human clemency, which in any case does not last. A wife, neither intelligent nor good but with her secret feelings, according to her indirect third-person self-assessment, has just recovered from some mysterious ailment, which she refers to, ominously, as an extravagance. This wife, tempted by Christ, by genius, by "extreme beauty," decides the bouquet of roses she's bought for herself are a danger, and pawns them off on a friend, only to regret this forfeiture.

"The one who understands disrupts," we are told in "Mineirinho." "There is something in us that would disrupt everything—a thing that understands." The story is about a man who has killed and is assassinated, in turn. "In killing this cornered man, she writes, "they do not kill him in us. Because I know that he is my error." Lispector digs under received notions of good and bad, of the gentle and the violent. "Everything that was violence in him is furtive in us." Underneath Mineirinho's act is a pure energy that is "dangerous as a gram of radium," a potentiality that can curdle and in Minheirinho "became a knife." The musings in this story on the nature of justice and charity are of an extraordinary depth. The one who understands disrupts. Lispector ponders the possibility of a killer inside her and declares that's not it, and instead, what's in us is this radium, which in Minheirinho, "caught fire." She calls for a justice that would examine itself, that "does not forget that we are all dangerous."

In "The Smallest Woman in the World," a family reads an article about a pygmy woman and pities her, but no more foolishly than the explorer who has "discovered" this woman, who pities him in turn. A little girl with purple circles under her eyes, in "The Foreign Legion," keeps intruding upon the writer who lives next door, her little girl pride a majestic absurdity the writer must somehow maneuver around, in the space of her own apartment. (This little girl, named Ofélia, reminds me so strongly of imperious young Lila in Elena Ferrante's novels, that I'm convinced Ferrante is influenced by Lispector, and why not? What could be better?) In "Remnants of Carnival," a different if equally intense and prideful little girl has aspirations to be a rose in the costumed public procession, to give an impression that will match her desires and mask the childhood she wants to reject. In "He Drank Me Up," a woman and her male makeup artist compete for the attentions of a metals magnate in a Mercedes. In this competition, the woman becomes convinced that her makeup artist is erasing her face, in order to drain her powers. She slaps herself back into reality, looks in the mirror, declares herself reborn.

Masks, makeup, domestic rooms that give way to the void: Appearances, Clarice helps us to understand, are not "mere," and instead critical, because they serve to cover the inscrutable deep. Lispector herself apparently had "permanent makeup" applied near the end of her life (she died at fifty-six, the age I will be tomorrow). I believe this turn to permanent makeup has meaning. A finally fixed visage is a kind of privacy, within which her interior work of introspecting could stay secret.

That work continues now. If makeup distracts from flaws, literature masks mortality. A writer who speaks the truth lives forever. This might be the case for a few, the great seers, and yet with none do I feel it so keenly as I do with Clarice (if I may be so bold). Because even as she does not mean to comfort, I feel her—here, still right *here*, to tell us how it really is.

RACHEL KUSHNER

OCTOBER 2024

ix

Love
("Amor")

A LITTLE TIRED, THE GROCERIES STRETCHING OUT HER new knit sack, Ana boarded the tram. She placed the bundle in her lap and the tram began to move. She then settled back in her seat trying to get comfortable, with a half-contented sigh.

Ana's children were good, something true and succulent. They were growing up, taking their baths, demanding for themselves, misbehaved, ever more complete moments. The kitchen was after all spacious, the faulty stove gave off small explosions. The heat was stifling in the apartment they were paying off bit by bit. But the wind whipping the curtains she herself had cut to measure reminded her that if she wanted she could stop and wipe her brow, gazing at the calm horizon. Like a farmhand. She had sown the seeds she held in her hand, no others, but these alone. And trees were growing. Her brief conversation with the electric bill collector was growing, the water in the laundry sink was growing, her children were growing, the table with food was growing, her husband coming home with the newspapers and smiling with hunger, the tiresome singing of the maids in the building. Ana gave to everything, tranquilly, her small, strong hand, her stream of life.

A certain hour of the afternoon was more dangerous. A certain hour of the afternoon the trees she had planted would laugh at her. When nothing else needed her strength, she got worried. Yet she felt more solid than ever, her body had filled out a bit and it was a sight to see her cut the fabric for the boys' shirts, the large scissors snapping on the cloth. All her vaguely artistic desire had long since been directed toward making the days fulfilled and beautiful; over time, her taste for the decorative had developed and supplanted her inner disorder. She seemed to have discovered that everything could be perfected, to each thing she could lend a harmonious appearance; life could be wrought by the hand of man.

Deep down, Ana had always needed to feel the firm root of things. And this is what a home bewilderingly had given her. Through winding paths, she had fallen into a woman's fate, with the surprise of fitting into it as if she had invented it. The man she'd married was a real man, the children she'd had were real children. Her former youth seemed as strange to her as one of life's illnesses. She had gradually emerged from it to discover that one could also live without happiness: abolishing it, she had found a legion of people, previously invisible, who lived the way a person works—with persistence, continuity, joy. What had happened to Ana before she had a home was forever out of reach: a restless exaltation so often mistaken for unbearable happiness. In exchange she had created something at last comprehensible, an adult life. That was what she had wanted and chosen.

The only thing she worried about was being careful during that dangerous hour of the afternoon, when the house was empty and needed nothing more from her, the sun high, the family members scattered to their duties. As she looked at the clean furniture, her heart would contract slightly in astonishment. But there was no room in her life for feeling tender toward her astonishment—she'd smother it with the same skill the household chores had given her. Then she'd go do the shopping or get something repaired, caring for her home and family in their absence. When she returned it would be the end of the afternoon and the children home from school needed her. In this way night would fall, with its peaceful vibration. In the morning she'd awake haloed by her calm duties. She'd find the furniture dusty and dirty again, as if repentantly come home. As for herself, she obscurely participated in the gentle black roots of the world. And nourished life anonymously. That was what she had wanted and chosen.

The tram went swaying along the tracks, heading down broad avenues. Soon a more humid breeze blew announcing, more than the end of the afternoon, the end of the unstable hour. Ana breathed deeply and a great acceptance gave her face a womanly air.

The tram would slow, then come to a halt. There was time to relax before Humaitá. That was when she looked at the man standing at the tram stop.

The difference between him and the others was that he really was stopped. Standing there, his hands reaching in front of him. He was blind.

What else could have made Ana sit up warily? Something uneasy was happening. Then she saw: the blind man was chewing gum ... A blind man was chewing gum.

Ana still had a second to think about how her brothers were coming for dinner—her heart beat violently, at intervals. Leaning forward, she stared intently at the blind man, the way we stare at things that don't see us. He was chewing gum in the dark. Without suffering, eyes open. The chewing motion made it look like he was smiling and then suddenly not smiling, smiling and not smiling—as if he had insulted her, Ana stared at him. And whoever saw her would have the impression of a woman filled with hatred. But she kept staring at him, leaning further and further forward—the tram suddenly lurched throwing her unexpectedly backward, the heavy knit sack tumbled from her lap, crashed to the floor—Ana screamed, the conductor gave the order to stop before he knew what was happening—the tram ground to a halt, the passengers looked around frightened.

Unable to move to pick up her groceries, Ana sat up, pale. A facial expression, long unused, had reemerged with difficulty, still tentative, incomprehensible. The paperboy laughed while returning her bundle. But the eggs had broken inside their newspaper wrapping. Viscous, yellow yolks dripped through the mesh. The blind man had interrupted his chewing and was reaching out his uncertain hands, trying in vain to grasp what was happening. The package of eggs had been thrown from the bag and, amid the passengers' smiles and the conductor's signal, the tram lurched back into motion.

A few seconds later nobody was looking at her. The tram rumbled along the tracks and the blind man chewing gum stayed behind forever. But the damage was done.

The knit mesh was rough between her fingers, not intimate as when she had knit it. The mesh had lost its meaning and being on a tram was a snapped thread; she didn't know what to do with the groceries on her lap. And like a strange song, the world started up again all around. The damage was done. Why? could she have forgotten there were blind people? Compassion was suffocating her, Ana breathed heavily. Even the things that existed before this event were now wary, had a more hostile, perishable aspect … The world had become once again a distress. Several years were crashing down, the yellow yolks were running. Expelled from her own days, she sensed that the people on the street were in peril, kept afloat on the surface of the darkness by a minimal balance—and for a moment the lack of meaning left them so free they didn't know where to go. The perception of an absence of law happened so suddenly that Ana clutched the seat in front of her, as if she might fall off the tram, as if things could be reverted with the same calm they no longer held.

What she called a crisis had finally come. And its sign was the intense pleasure with which she now looked at things, suffering in alarm. The heat had become more stifling, everything had gained strength and louder voices. On the Rua Voluntários da Pátria a revolution seemed about to break out, the sewer grates were dry, the air dusty. A blind man chewing gum had plunged the world into dark voraciousness. In every strong person there was an absence of compassion for the blind man and people frightened her with the vigor they possessed. Next to her was a lady in blue, with a face. She averted her gaze, quickly. On the sidewalk, a woman shoved her son! Two lovers interlaced their fingers smiling … And the blind man? Ana had fallen into an excruciating benevolence.

She had pacified life so well, taken such care for it not to explode. She had kept it all in serene comprehension, separated each person from the rest, clothes were clearly made to be worn and you could choose the evening movie from the newspaper—everything wrought in such a way that one day followed another. And a blind man chewing gum was shattering it all to pieces. And through this compassion there appeared to Ana a life full of sweet nausea, rising to her mouth.

Only then did she realize she was long past her stop. In her weak state everything was hitting her with a jolt; she left the tram weak in the knees, looked around, clutching the egg-stained mesh. For a moment she couldn't get her bearings. She seemed to have stepped off into the middle of the night.

It was a long street, with high, yellow walls. Her heart pounding with fear, she sought in vain to recognize her surroundings, while the life she had discovered kept pulsating and a warmer, more mysterious wind whirled round her face. She stood there looking at the wall. At last she figured out where she was. Walking a little further along a hedge, she passed through the gates of the Botanical Garden.

She trudged down the central promenade, between the coconut palms. There was no one in the Garden. She put her packages on the ground, sat on a bench along a path and stayed there a long while.

The vastness seemed to calm her, the silence regulated her breathing. She was falling asleep inside herself.

From a distance she saw the avenue of palms where the afternoon was bright and full. But the shade of the branches covered the path.

All around were serene noises, scent of trees, little surprises among the vines. The whole Garden crushed by the ever faster instants of the afternoon. From where did that half-dream come that encircled her? Like a droning of bees and birds. Everything was strange, too gentle, too big.

A light, intimate movement startled her—she spun around. Nothing seemed to have moved. But motionless in the central avenue stood a powerful cat. Its fur was soft. Resuming its silent walk, it disappeared.

Worried, she looked around. The branches were swaying,

the shadows wavering on the ground. A sparrow was pecking at the dirt. And suddenly, in distress, she seemed to have fallen into an ambush. There was a secret labor underway in the Garden that she was starting to perceive.

In the trees the fruits were black, sweet like honey. On the ground were dried pits full of circumvolutions, like little rotting brains. The bench was stained with purple juices. With intense gentleness the waters murmured. Clinging to the tree trunk were the luxuriant limbs of a spider. The cruelty of the world was tranquil. The murder was deep. And death was not what we thought.

While imaginary—it was a world to sink one's teeth into, a world of voluminous dahlias and tulips. The trunks were crisscrossed by leafy parasites, their embrace was soft, sticky. Like the revulsion that precedes a surrender—it was fascinating, the woman was nauseated, and it was fascinating.

The trees were laden, the world was so rich it was rotting. When Ana thought how there were children and grown men going hungry, the nausea rose to her throat, as if she were pregnant and abandoned. The moral of the Garden was something else. Now that the blind man had led her to it, she trembled upon the first steps of a sparkling, shadowy world, where giant water lilies floated monstrous. The little flowers scattered through the grass didn't look yellow or rosy to her, but the color of bad gold and scarlet. The decomposition was deep, perfumed … But all the heavy things, she saw with her head encircled by a swarm of insects, sent by the most exquisite life in the world. The breeze insinuated itself among the flowers. Ana sensed rather than smelled its sweetish scent … The Garden was so pretty that she was afraid of Hell.

It was nearly evening now and everything seemed full, heavy, a squirrel leaped in the shadows. Beneath her feet the earth was soft, Ana inhaled it with delight. It was fascinating, and she felt nauseated.

But when she remembered the children, toward whom she was now guilty, she stood with a cry of pain. She grabbed her bag, went down the dark path, reached the promenade. She was nearly running—and she saw the Garden all around, with its haughty impersonality. She rattled the locked gates, rattled them gripping the rough wood. The guard appeared, shocked not to have seen her.

Until she reached the door of her building, she seemed on the verge of a disaster. She ran to the elevator clutching the mesh sack, her soul pounding in her chest—what was happening? Her compassion for the blind man was as violent as an agony, but the world seemed to be hers, dirty, perishable, hers. She opened her front door. The living room was large, square, the doorknobs were gleaming spotlessly, the window-panes gleaming, the lamp gleaming—what new land was this? And for an instant the wholesome life she had led up till now seemed like a morally insane way to live. The boy who ran to her was a being with long legs and a face just like hers, who ran up and hugged her. She clutched him tightly, in alarm. She protected herself trembling. Because life was in peril. She loved the world, loved what had been created—she loved with nausea. The same way she'd always been fascinated by oysters, with that vaguely sick feeling she always got when nearing the truth, warning her. She embraced her son, nearly to the point of hurting him. As if she had learned of an evil—the blind man or the lovely Botanical Garden?—she clung to him, whom she loved more than anything. She had been touched by the demon of faith. Life is horrible, she said to him softly, ravenous. What would she do if she heeded the call of the blind man? She would go alone … There were places poor and rich that needed her. She needed them … I'm scared, she said. She felt the child's delicate ribs between her arms, heard his frightened sobbing. Mama, the boy called. She held him away from her, looked at that face, her heart cringed. Don't let Mama forget you, she told him. As soon as the child felt her embrace loosen, he broke free and fled to the bedroom door, looking at her from greater safety. It was the worst look she had ever received. The blood rushed to her face, warming it.

She let herself fall into a chair, her fingers still gripping the mesh sack. What was she ashamed of?

There was no escape. The days she had forged had ruptured the crust and the water was pouring out. She was facing the oyster. And there was no way not to look at it. What was she ashamed of? That it was no longer compassion, it wasn't just compassion: her heart had filled with the worst desire to live.

She no longer knew whether she was on the side of the blind man or the dense plants. The man had gradually receded into the distance and in torture she seemed to have gone over to the side of whoever had wounded his eyes. The Botanical Garden, tranquil and tall, was revealing this to her. In horror she was discovering that she belonged to the strong part of the world—and what name should she give her violent mercy? She would have to kiss the leper, since she would never be just his sister. A blind man led me to the worst in myself, she thought in alarm. She felt banished because no pauper would drink water from her ardent hands. Ah! it was easier to be a saint than a person! By God, hadn't it been real, the compassion that had fathomed the deepest waters of her heart? But it was the compassion of a lion.

Humiliated, she knew the blind man would prefer a poorer love. And, trembling, she also knew why. The life of the Botanical Garden was calling her as a werewolf is called by the moonlight. Oh! but she loved the blind man! she thought with moist eyes. Yet this wasn't the feeling you'd go to church with. I'm scared, she said alone in the living room. She got up and went to the kitchen to help the maid with dinner.

But life made her shiver, like a chill. She heard the school bell, distant and constant. The little horror of the dust threading together the bottom of the stove, where she discovered the little spider. Carrying the vase to change its water—there was the horror of the flower surrendering languid and sickening to her hands. The same secret labor was underway there in the kitchen. Near the trash can, she crushed the ant with her foot. The little murder of the ant. The tiny body trembled. The water droplets were dripping into the stagnant water in the laundry sink. The summer beetles. The horror of the inexpressive beetles. All around was a silent, slow, persistent life. Horror, horror. She paced back and forth across the kitchen, slicing the steaks, stirring the sauce. Round her head, circling, round the light, the mosquitoes of a sweltering night. A night on which compassion was raw as bad love. Between her two breasts sweat slid down. Faith was breaking her, the heat from the oven stung her eyes.

Then her husband arrived, her brothers and their wives arrived, her brothers' children arrived.

They ate dinner with all the windows open, on the ninth floor. An airplane went shuddering past, threatening in the heat of the sky. Though made with not enough eggs, the dinner was good. Her children stayed up too, playing on the rug with the others. It was summer, it would be pointless to send them to bed. Ana was a little pale and laughed softly with the others.

After dinner, at last, the first cooler breeze came in through the windows. They sat around the table, the family. Worn out from the day, glad not to disagree, so ready not to find fault. They laughed at everything, with kind and human hearts. The children were growing up admirably around them. And as if it were a butterfly, Ana caught the instant between her fingers before it was never hers again.

Later, when everyone had gone and the children were already in bed, she was a brute woman looking out the window. The city was asleep and hot. Would whatever the blind man had unleashed fit into her days? How many years would it take for her to grow old again? The slightest movement and she'd trample one of the children. But with a lover's mischief, she seemed to accept that out of the flower emerged the mosquito, that the giant water lilies floated on the darkness of the lake. The blind man dangled among the fruits of the Botanical Garden.

If that was the stove exploding, the whole house would already be on fire! she thought rushing into the kitchen and finding her husband in front of the spilled coffee.

"What happened?!" she screamed vibrating all over.

He jumped at his wife's fright. And suddenly laughed in comprehension:

"It was nothing," he said, "I'm just clumsy." He looked tired, bags under his eyes.

But encountering Ana's strange face, he peered at her with greater attention. Then he drew her close, in a swift caress.

"I don't want anything to happen to you, ever!" she said.

"At least let the stove explode at me," he answered smiling.

She stayed limp in his arms. This afternoon something

tranquil had burst, and a humorous, sad tone was hanging over the house. "Time for bed," he said, "it's late." In a gesture that wasn't his, but that seemed natural, he held his wife's hand, taking her along without looking back, removing her from the danger of living.

The dizziness of benevolence was over.

And, if she had passed through love and its hell, she was now combing her hair before the mirror, for an instant with no world at all in her heart. Before going to bed, as if putting out a candle, she blew out the little flame of the day.

A Chicken
("Uma galinha")

SHE WAS A SUNDAY CHICKEN. STILL ALIVE BECAUSE IT wasn't yet nine in the morning.

She seemed calm. Since Saturday she'd been huddling in a corner of the kitchen. She looked at no one, no one looked at her. Even when they selected her, feeling up her intimate parts indifferently, they couldn't tell whether she was fat or skinny. No one would ever guess she had a yearning.

So it came as a surprise when they saw her flap her wings made for brief flight, puff up her chest and, in two or three bursts, reach the terrace railing. For a second she wavered— long enough for the cook to cry out—and soon was on the neighbor's terrace, from which, in another awkward flight, she reached a roof. There she stood like an out-of-place ornament, hesitating on one foot, then the other. The family was urgently summoned and in dismay saw their lunch by a chimney. The man of the house, recalling the dual need to engage sporadically in some kind of sport and to have lunch, gleefully donned a pair of swim trunks and decided to follow in the chicken's path: with cautious leaps he reached the roof where she, hesitant and trembling, was urgently determining a further route.

The chase intensified. From rooftop to rooftop they covered more than a block. Ill-adapted to a wilder struggle for life, the chicken had to decide for herself which way to go, without any help from her race. The young man, however, was a dormant hunter. And inconsequential as the prey was, the rallying cry had sounded.

Alone in the world, without father or mother, she ran, panting, mute, focused. At times, mid-escape, she'd flutter breathlessly on the eave of a roof and while the young man went stumbling across other roofs she'd have time to gather herself for a moment. And then she seemed so free.

Stupid, timid and free. Not victorious as an escaping rooster would have been. What was it in her guts that made her a being? The chicken is a being. It's true you couldn't count on her for anything. Even she didn't count on herself for anything, as the rooster believes in his comb. Her sole advantage was that there were so many chickens that whenever one died another emerged that very instant as alike as if it were the same.

Finally, on one of her pauses to revel in her escape, the young man reached her. Amid cries and feathers, she was caught. Then carried triumphantly by one wing across the rooftops and placed on the kitchen floor with a certain violence. Still dizzy, she shook herself a little, clucking hoarsely and uncertainly.

That's when it happened. Completely frantic the chicken laid an egg. Surprised, exhausted. Perhaps it was premature. But right after, born as she was for maternity, she looked like an old, experienced mother. She sat on the egg and stayed there, breathing, her eyes buttoning up and unbuttoning. Her heart, so small on a plate, made her feathers rise and fall, filling with warmth a thing that would never be more than an egg. The little girl was the only one nearby and watched everything in terror. Yet as soon as she managed to tear herself away, she pried herself off the floor and ran shouting:

"Mama, Mama, don't kill the chicken anymore, she laid an egg! she cares about us!"

Everyone ran back into the kitchen and wordlessly surrounded the youthful new mother. Warming her offspring, she was neither gentle nor standoffish, neither cheerful nor sad, she was nothing, she was a chicken. Which wouldn't suggest any special feeling. The father, the mother and the daughter had been staring for quite some time, without thinking anything in particular. No one had ever petted a chicken's head before. The father finally made up his mind somewhat abruptly:

"If you have this chicken killed I'll never eat chicken again for the rest of my life!"

"Me neither!" vowed the girl ardently.

The mother, tired, shrugged.

Unconscious of the life she had been granted, the chicken began living with the family. The girl, coming home from school, would fling her binder down without missing a beat in her dash to the kitchen. Occasionally the father would recall: "And to think I made her run in that condition!" The chicken had become queen of the house. Everyone, except her, knew it. She carried on between the kitchen and the back terrace, employing her twin talents: apathy and alarm.

But whenever everyone in the house was quiet and seemed to have forgotten her, she would fill up with a little courage, vestiges of the great escape—and roam the tiled patio, her body following her head, pausing as if in a field, though her little head gave her away: vibratory and bobbing rapidly, the ancient fright of her species long since turned mechanical.

Every once in a while, though increasingly rarely, the chicken would again recall the figure she had cut against the air on the edge of the roof, about to proclaim herself. That's when she'd fill her lungs with the kitchen's sullied air and, even if females were given to crowing, wouldn't crow but would feel much happier. Though not even then would the expression change on her empty head. While fleeing, resting, giving birth or pecking corn—it was a chicken's head, the same one drawn at the start of the centuries.

Until one day they killed her, ate her and years went by.

The Imitation of the Rose
("A imitação da rosa")

BEFORE ARMANDO GOT HOME FROM WORK THE HOUSE had better be tidy and she already in her brown dress so she could tend to her husband while he got dressed, and then they'd leave calmly, arm in arm like the old days. How long since they had done that?

But now that she was "well" again, they'd take the bus, she gazing out the window like a wife, her arm in his, and then they'd have dinner with Carlota and João, reclining comfortably in their chairs. How long since she had seen Armando at last recline comfortably and have a conversation with a man? A man's peace lay in forgetting about his wife, discussing the latest headlines with another man. Meanwhile she'd chat with Carlota about women's stuff, giving in to Carlota's authoritative and practical benevolence, receiving again at last her friend's inattention and vague disdain, her natural bluntness, and no more of that perplexed and overly curious affection—and at last seeing Armando forget about his wife. And she herself, at last, returning gratefully to insignificance. Like a cat who stayed out all night and, as if nothing had happened, finds a saucer of milk waiting without a word. People were luckily helping her feel she was now "well." Without looking at her, they were actively helping her forget, pretending they themselves had forgotten as if they'd read the same label on the same medicine bottle. Or they really had forgotten, who knows. How long since she had seen Armando at last recline with abandon, forget about her? And as for her?

Breaking off from tidying the vanity, Laura looked at herself in the mirror: and as for her, how long had it been? Her face held a domestic charm, her hair was pinned back behind her large, pale ears. Her brown eyes, brown hair, her tawny, smooth skin, all this lent her no longer youthful face a modest, womanly air. Would anyone happen to see, in that tiniest point of surprise lodged in the depths of her eyes, would anyone see in that tiniest offended speck the lack of the children she'd never had?

With her meticulous penchant for method—the same that compelled her as a student to copy the lesson's main points in perfect handwriting without understanding them—with her penchant for method, now resumed, she was planning to tidy the house before the maid's day off so that, once Maria was gone, she wouldn't have to do anything else, except 1) calmly get dressed; 2) wait for Armando ready to go; 3) what was three? Right. That's exactly what she'd do. And she'd put on the brown dress with the cream lace collar. Already showered. Back at Sacré Coeur she'd been tidy and clean, with a penchant for personal hygiene and a certain horror of messiness. Which never made Carlota, already back then a bit original, admire her. Their reactions had always been different. Carlota ambitious and laughing heartily: she, Laura, a little slow, and as it were careful always to stay slow; Carlota not seeing the danger in anything. And she ever cautious. When they'd been assigned to read *The Imitation of Christ*, she'd read it with a fool's ardor without understanding but, God forgive her, she'd felt that whoever imitated Christ would be lost—lost in the light, but dangerously lost. Christ was the worst temptation. And Carlota hadn't even wanted to read it, she lied to the nun saying she had. Right. She'd put on the brown dress with the real lace collar.

But when she saw the time she remembered, with a jolt that made her lift her hand to her chest, that she'd forgotten to drink her glass of milk.

She went to the kitchen and, as if in her carelessness she'd guiltily betrayed Armando and her devoted friends, while still at the refrigerator she drank the first sips with an anxious slowing, concentrating on each sip faithfully as if making amends to them all and repenting. Since the doctor had said: "Drink milk between meals, avoid an empty stomach because it causes anxiety"—so, even without the threat of anxiety, she drank it without a fuss sip by sip, day after day, without fail, obeying with her eyes closed, with a slight ardor for not discerning the slightest skepticism in herself. The awkward thing was that the doctor seemed to contradict himself when, while giving a precise order that she wished to follow with a convert's zeal, he'd also said: "Let yourself go, take it easy, don't strain yourself to make it work—forget all about what happened and everything will fall back into place naturally." And he patted her on the back, which flattered her and made her blush with pleasure. But in her humble opinion one order seemed to cancel the other, as if they'd asked her to eat flour and whistle at the same time. To combine them she'd recently resorted to a trick: the glass of milk that had ended up gaining a secret power, every sip of which contained the near-taste of a word and renewed that firm pat on the back, she'd take that glass of milk into the living room, where she'd sit "very naturally," pretending not to care at all, "not straining herself" — and thereby cleverly carrying out the second order. "It doesn't matter if I gain weight," she thought, looks had never been the point.

She sat on the sofa like a guest in her own house that, so recently regained, tidy and cool, evoked the tranquility of someone else's house. Which was so satisfying: unlike Carlota, who had made of her home something akin to herself, Laura took such pleasure in making her house an impersonal thing; somehow perfect for being impersonal.

Oh how good it was to be back, really back, she smiled in satisfaction. Holding the nearly empty glass, she closed her eyes with a sigh of pleasant fatigue. She'd ironed Armando's shirts, drawn up methodical lists for the next day, minutely calculated how much she'd spent at the market that morning, hadn't stopped in fact for even a second. Oh how good it was to be tired again.

If a perfect person from the planet Mars landed and discovered that Earthlings got tired and grew old, that person would feel pity and astonishment. Without ever understanding what was good about being human, in feeling tired, in giving out daily; only the initiated would comprehend this subtlety of defectiveness and this refinement of life.

And she'd finally returned from the perfection of the planet Mars. She, who had never cherished any ambition besides being a man's wife, was gratefully reencountering the part of her that gave out daily. With her eyes shut she sighed in appreciation. How long since she had got tired? But now every day she felt nearly exhausted and had ironed, for example, Armando's shirts, she'd always enjoyed ironing and, modesty aside, had a knack for it. And then she'd be exhausted as a reward. No longer that alert lack of fatigue. No longer that empty and wakeful and horribly marvelous speck inside her. No longer that terrible independence. No longer the monstrous and simple ease of not sleeping—day or night—which in its discreet way had made her suddenly superhuman compared to a tired and perplexed husband. He, with that bad breath he got whenever he went mute with worry, which gave her a pungent compassion, yes, even within her wakeful perfection, compassion and love, she superhuman and tranquil in her gleaming isolation, and he, whenever he'd come to visit timidly bearing apples and grapes that the nurse would eat with a shrug, he paying formal visits like a boyfriend, with his unfortunate bad breath and stiff smile, straining heroically to comprehend, he who had received her from a father and a priest, and had no idea what to do with this girl from Tijuca who had unexpectedly, as a tranquil boat bursts into sail on the waters, become superhuman.

Now, no more of this. Never again. Oh, it had just been a bout of weakness; genius was the worst temptation. But afterward she'd returned so completely that she'd even had to start being careful again not to wear people down with her old penchant for detail. She clearly remembered her classmates at Sacré Coeur saying to her: "You've told it a thousand times!" she recalled with an embarrassed smile. She'd returned so completely: now she got tired every day, every day her face would sag at dusk, and then night would take on its former purpose, it wasn't just the perfect starlit night. And everything lined up harmoniously. And, as with everyone else, each day wore her out; like everyone else, human and perishable. No longer that perfection, no longer that youth. No longer that thing that one day had spread brightly, like a cancer, to her soul.

She opened her sleep-laden eyes, feeling the nice solid glass in her hands, but closed them again with a comfortable smile of fatigue, bathing like some nouveau riche in all her particles, in that familiar and slightly nauseating water. Yes, slightly nauseating; what did it matter, since she too was a bit nauseating, she was well aware. But her husband didn't think so, and so what did it matter, since thank God she didn't live in an environment that required her to be more clever and interesting, and she'd even freed herself from high school, which had so awkwardly demanded that she stay alert. What did it matter. In fatigue—she'd ironed Armando's shirts, not to mention she'd gone to the farmers' market that morning and lingered there so long, with that pleasure she took in making the most of things—in fatigue there was a nice place for her, the discreet and dulled place from which, so embarrassingly for herself and everyone else, she had once emerged. But, as she kept saying, thank God, she'd returned.

And if she sought with greater faith and love, she would find within her fatigue that even better place called sleep. She sighed with pleasure, in a moment of spiteful mischief tempted to go along with that warm exhalation that was her already somnolent breathing, tempted to doze off for a second. "Just a second, just one little second!" she begged herself, flattered to be so drowsy, begging pleadingly, as if begging a man, which Armando had always liked.

But she didn't really have time to sleep now, not even for a quick nap—she thought vainly and with false modesty, she was such a busy person! She'd always envied people who said "I didn't have time" and now she was once again such a busy person: they were going to Carlota's for dinner and everything had to be orderly and ready, it was her first dinner party since coming back and she didn't want to be late, she had to be ready when … right, I've already said it a thousand times, she thought sheepishly. Once was enough to say: "I don't want to be late"—since that reason sufficed: if she had never been able to bear without the utmost mortification being a nuisance to anyone, then now, more than ever, she shouldn't … No, there wasn't the slightest doubt: she didn't have time to sleep. What she ought to do, familiarly slipping into that intimate wealth of routine—and it hurt her that Carlota scoffed at her penchant for routine—what she ought to do was 1) wait till the maid was ready; 2) give her money to get meat in the morning, rump roast; how could she explain that the difficulty of finding quality meat really was a good topic of conversation, but if Carlota found out she'd scoff at her; 3) start meticulously showering and getting dressed, fully surrendering to the pleasure of making the most of her time. That brown dress complemented her eyes and its little cream lace collar gave her a childlike quality, like an old-fashioned boy. And, back to the nocturnal peace of Tijuca—no longer that blinding light from those coiffed and perky nurses leaving for their day off after tossing her like a helpless chicken into the abyss of insulin—back to the nocturnal peace of Tijuca, back to her real life: she'd go arm-in-arm with Armando, walking slowly to the bus stop, with those short, thick thighs packed into that girdle making her a "woman of distinction"; but whenever, upset, she told Armando it was because of an ovarian insufficiency, he, who took pride in his wife's thighs, replied rather cheekily: "What would I get out of marrying a ballerina?" that was how he replied. You'd never guess, but Armando could sometimes be really naughty, you'd never guess. Once in a while they said the same thing. She'd explain that it was because of an ovarian insufficiency. So then he'd say: "What would I get out of marrying a ballerina?" He could be really shameless sometimes, you'd never guess. Carlota would be astonished to learn that they too had a private life and things they never told, but she wouldn't tell, what a shame not to be able to tell, Carlota definitely thought she was just uptight and mundane and a little annoying, and if she had to be careful not to bother other people with details, with Armando she'd sometimes relax and get pretty annoying, which didn't matter because he'd pretend to be listening without really listening to everything she was telling him, which didn't hurt her feelings, she understood perfectly well that her chatter tired people out a bit, but it was nice to be able to explain how she hadn't found any meat even if Armando shook his head and wasn't listening, she and the maid chatted a lot, actually she talked more than the maid, and she was also careful not to pester the maid who sometimes held back her impatience and could get a little rude, it was her own fault because she didn't always command respect.

But, as she was saying, her arm in his, she so short and he tall and slim, but he was healthy thank God, and she a brunette. She was a brunette as she obscurely believed a wife ought to be. To have black or blonde hair was an excess to which she, in her desire to do everything right, had never aspired. Therefore, as for green eyes, it seemed to her that having green eyes would be like keeping certain things from her husband. Not that Carlota exactly gave her reason to gossip, but she, Laura—who if given the chance would defend her fervently, but never got the chance—she, Laura, grudgingly had to agree that her friend had a peculiar and funny way of dealing with her husband, oh not that she acted "as if they were equals," as people were doing nowadays, but you know what I mean. And Carlota was even a bit original, she'd even mentioned this once to Armando and Armando had agreed but hadn't thought it mattered much. But, as she was saying, dressed in brown with her little collar … —this daydream was filling her with the same pleasure she got from tidying drawers, sometimes she'd even mess them up just to be able to tidy them again.

She opened her eyes, and as if the room had dozed off instead of her, it seemed refreshed and relaxed with its brushed armchairs and the curtains that had shrunk in the last wash, like pants that were too short while the person stood comically peering down at his legs. Oh how nice it was to see everything tidy and dusted again, everything cleaned by her own skillful hands, and so silent, and with a vase full of flowers, like a waiting room. She'd always found waiting rooms lovely, so courteous, so impersonal. How rich normal life was, she who had returned from extravagance at last. Even a vase of flowers. She looked at it.

"Oh they're so lovely," her heart exclaimed suddenly a bit childish. They were small wild roses she'd bought at the farmers' market that morning, partly because the man had been so insistent, partly out of daring. She'd arranged them in the vase that very morning, while drinking her sacred ten o'clock glass of milk.

Yet bathed in the light of this room the roses stood in all their complete and tranquil beauty.

I've never seen such pretty roses, she thought with curiosity. And as if she hadn't just had that exact thought, vaguely aware that she'd just had that exact thought and quickly glossing over the awkwardness of realizing she was being a little tedious, she thought in a further stage of surprise: "Honestly, I've never seen such pretty roses." She looked at them attentively. But her attention couldn't remain mere attention for long, it soon was transformed into gentle pleasure, and she couldn't manage to keep analyzing the roses, she had to interrupt herself with the same exclamation of submissive curiosity: they're so lovely.

They were some perfect roses, several on the same stem. At some point they'd climbed over one another with nimble eagerness but then, once the game was over, they had tranquilly stopped moving. They were some roses so perfect in their smallness, not entirely in bloom, and their pinkish hue was nearly white. They even look fake! she said in surprise. They might look white if they were completely open but, with their central petals curled into buds, their color was concentrated and, as inside an earlobe, you could feel the redness coursing through them. They're so lovely, thought Laura in surprise.

But without knowing why, she was a little embarrassed, a little disturbed. Oh, not too much, it was just that extreme beauty made her uncomfortable.

She heard the maid's footsteps on the kitchen tile and could tell from the hollow sound that she was wearing heels; so she must be ready to leave. Then Laura had a somewhat original idea: why not ask Maria to stop by Carlota's and leave her the roses as a present?

And also because that extreme beauty made her uncomfortable. Uncomfortable? It was a risk. Oh, no, why would it be a risk? They just made her uncomfortable, they were a warning, oh no, why would they be a warning? Maria would give Carlota the roses.

"Dona Laura sent them," Maria would say.

She smiled thoughtfully: Carlota would think it odd that Laura, who could bring the roses herself, since she wanted to give them as a present, sent them with the maid before dinner. Not to mention she'd find it amusing to get roses, she'd think it "refined" …

"There's no need for things like that between us, Laura!" her friend would say with that slightly rude bluntness, and Laura would exclaim in a muffled cry of rapture:

"Oh no! no! It's not because you invited us to dinner! it's just that the roses were so lovely I decided on a whim to give them to you!"

Yes, if when the time came she could find a way and got the nerve, that's exactly what she'd say. How was it again that she'd say it? she mustn't forget: she'd say—"Oh no!" etc. And Carlota would be surprised by the delicacy of Laura's feelings, no one would ever imagine that Laura too had her little ideas. In this imaginary and agreeable scene that made her smile beatifically, she called herself "Laura," as if referring to a third person. A third person full of that gentle and crackling and grateful and tranquil faith, Laura, the one with the little real-lace collar, discreetly dressed, Armando's wife, finally an Armando who no longer needed to force himself to pay attention to all of her chattering about the maid and meat, who no longer needed to think about his wife, like a man who is happy, like a man who isn't married to a ballerina.

"I couldn't help but send you the roses," Laura would say, that third person so, so very … And giving the roses was nearly as lovely as the roses themselves.

And indeed she'd be rid of them.

And what indeed would happen then? Ah, yes: as she was saying, Carlota surprised by that Laura who was neither intelligent nor good but who also had her secret feelings. And Armando? Armando would look at her with a healthy dose of astonishment—since you can't forget there's no possible way for him to know that the maid brought the roses this afternoon!—Armando would look fondly on the whims of his little woman, and that night they'd sleep together.

And she'd have forgotten the roses and their beauty.

No, she thought suddenly vaguely forewarned. She must watch out for other people's alarmed stares. She must never again give cause for alarm, especially with everything still so recent. And most important of all was sparing everyone from suffering the least bit of doubt. And never again cause other people to fuss over her—never again that awful thing where everyone stared at her mutely, and her right there in front of everyone. No whims.

But at the same time she saw the empty glass of milk in her hand and also thought: "he" said not to strain myself to make it work, not to worry about acting a certain way just to prove that I'm already ...

"Maria," she then said upon hearing the maid's footsteps again. And when Maria approached, she said impetuously and defiantly: "Could you stop by Dona Carlota's and leave these roses for her? Say it like this: 'Dona Carlota, Dona Laura sent these.' Say it like this: 'Dona Carlota ...'"

"Got it, got it," said the maid patiently.

Laura went to find an old piece of tissue paper. Then she carefully took the roses out of the vase, so lovely and tranquil, with their delicate and deadly thorns. She wanted to give the arrangement an artistic touch. And at the same time be rid of them. And she could get dressed and move on with her day. When she gathered the moist little roses into a bouquet, she extended the hand holding them, looked at them from a distance, tilting her head and narrowing her eyes for an impartial and severe judgment.

And when she looked at them, she saw the roses.

And then, stubborn, gentle, she coaxed inwardly: don't give away the roses, they're lovely.

A second later, still very gentle, the thought intensified slightly, almost tantalizing: don't give them away, they're yours. Laura gasped a little: because things were never hers.

But these roses were. Rosy, small, perfect: hers. She looked at them in disbelief: they were beautiful and hers. If she managed to think further, she'd think: hers like nothing else had ever been.

And she could even keep them since she'd already shed that initial discomfort that made her vaguely avoid looking at the roses too much.

Why give them away, then? lovely and you're giving them away? After all when you happen upon a good thing, you just go and give it away? After all if they were hers, she coaxed persuasively without finding any argument besides the one that, with repetition, seemed increasingly convincing and simple. They wouldn't last long—so why give them away while they were still alive? The pleasure of having them didn't pose much of a risk— she deluded herself—after all, whether or not she wanted them, she'd have to give them up soon enough, and then she'd never think of them again since they'd be dead—they wouldn't last long, so why give them away? The fact that they didn't last long seemed to remove her guilt about keeping them, according to the obscure logic of a woman who sins. After all you could see they wouldn't last long (it would be quick, free from danger). And besides—she argued in a final and triumphant rejection of guilt—by no means had she been the one who'd wanted to buy them, the vendor kept insisting and she always got so flustered when people put her on the spot, she hadn't been the one who'd wanted to buy them, she was in no way to blame whatsoever. She looked at them entranced, thoughtful, profound.

And, honestly, I've never seen anything more perfect in all my life.

Fine, but now she'd already spoken to Maria and there was no way to turn back. So was it too late?, she got scared, seeing the little roses waiting impassively in her own hand. If she wanted, it wouldn't be too late … She could tell Maria: "Listen Maria, I've decided to take the roses over myself when I go to dinner!" And, of course, she wouldn't take them … And Maria would never have to know. And, before changing clothes, she'd sit on the sofa for a second, just a second, to look at them. And to look at those roses' tranquil detachment. Yes, since, having done the deed, you might as well take advantage of it, wouldn't it be silly to take the blame without reaping the rewards. That's exactly what she'd do.

But with the unwrapped roses in her hand she waited. She wasn't putting them back in the vase, she wasn't calling Maria. She knew why. Because she ought to give them away. Oh she knew why.

And also because a pretty thing was meant for giving or receiving, not just having. And, above all, never just for "being." Above all one should never be the pretty thing. A pretty thing lacked the gesture of giving. One should never keep a pretty thing, just like that, as if stowed inside the perfect silence of the heart. (Although, if she didn't give away the roses, no one in the world would ever know that she'd planned to give them away, who would ever find out? it was horribly easy and doable to keep them, since who would ever find out? and they'd be hers, and that would be the end of it and no one would mention it again …)

So? and so? she wondered vaguely worried.

So, no. What she ought to do was wrap them up and send them off, without any enjoyment now; wrap them up and, disappointed, send them off; and in astonishment be rid of them. Also because a person must have some consistency, her thinking ought to have some continuity: if she'd spontaneously decided to hand them over to Carlota, she should stick to her decision and give them away. Because no one changed their mind from one moment to the next.

But anyone can have regrets! she suddenly rebelled. Since it was only the moment I picked the roses up that I realized how beautiful I thought they were, for the very first time in fact, when I picked them up, that's when I realized they were beautiful. Or just before? (And besides they were hers). And besides the doctor himself had patted her on the back and said: "Don't strain to pretend you're well, ma'am, because you *are* well," and then that firm pat on the back. That's why, then, she didn't have to be consistent, she didn't have to prove anything to anyone and she'd keep the roses. (And besides—besides they were hers).

"Are they ready?" asked Maria.

"Yes," said Laura caught by surprise.

She looked at them, so mute in her hand. Impersonal in their extreme beauty. In their extreme, perfect rose tranquility. That last resort: the flower. That final perfection: luminous tranquility.

Like an addict, she looked with faint greed at the roses' tantalizing perfection, with her mouth slightly dry she looked at them.

Until, slow, austere, she wrapped the stems and thorns in the tissue paper. She had been so absorbed that only when she held out the finished bouquet did she realize that Maria was no longer in the room—and she was left alone with her heroic sacrifice. Vaguely afflicted, she looked at them, remote at the end of her outstretched arm—and her mouth grew still more parched, that envy, that desire. But they're mine, she said with enormous timidity.

When Maria returned and took the bouquet, in a fleeting instant of greed Laura pulled her hand away keeping the roses one second longer—they're lovely and they're mine, it's the first thing that's lovely and mine! plus it was that man who insisted, it wasn't me who went looking for them! fate wanted it this way! oh just this once! just this once and I swear never again! (She could at least take one rose for herself, no more than that: one rose for herself. And only she would know, and then never again oh, she promised herself that never again would she let herself be tempted by perfection, never again!)

And the next second, without any transition at all, without any obstacle at all—the roses were in the maid's hand, they were no longer hers, like a letter already slipped into the mailbox! no more chances to take it back or cross anything out! it was no use crying: that's not what I meant! She was left empty-handed but her obstinate and resentful heart was still saying: "you can catch Maria on the stairs, you know perfectly well you can, and snatch the roses from her hand and steal them." Because taking them now would be stealing. Stealing something that was hers? Since that's what someone who felt no pity for others would do: steal something that was rightfully hers! Oh, have mercy, dear God. You can take it all back, she insisted furiously. And then the front door slammed.

Then the front door slammed.

Then slowly she sat calmly on the sofa. Without leaning back. Just to rest. No, she wasn't angry, oh not at all. But that offended speck in the depths of her eyes had grown larger and more pensive. She looked at the vase. "Where are my roses," she then said very calmly.

And she missed the roses. They had left a bright space inside her. Remove an object from a clean table and from the even cleaner mark it leaves you can see that dust had been surrounding it. The roses had left a dustless, sleepless space inside her. In her heart, that rose she could at least have taken for herself without hurting anyone in the world, was missing. Like some greater lack.

In fact, like the lack. An absence that was entering her like a brightness. And the dust was also disappearing from around the mark the roses left. The center of her fatigue was opening in an expanding circle. As if she hadn't ironed a single one of Armando's shirts. And in the clear space the roses were missed. "Where are my roses," she wailed without pain while smoothing the pleats in her skirt.

Like when you squeeze lemon into black tea and the black tea starts brightening all over. Her fatigue was gradually brightening. Without any fatigue whatsoever, incidentally. The way a firefly lights up. Since she was no longer tired, she'd get up and get dressed. It was time to start.

But, her lips dry, she tried for a second to imitate the roses inside herself. It wasn't even hard.

It was all the better that she wasn't tired. That way she'd go to dinner even more refreshed. Why not pin that cameo onto her little real-lace collar? that the major had brought back from the war in Italy. It would set off her neckline so nicely. When she was ready she'd hear the sound of Armando's key in the door. She needed to get dressed. But it was still early. He'd be caught in traffic. It was still afternoon. A very pretty afternoon.

Incidentally it was no longer afternoon.

It was night. From the street rose the first sounds of the darkness and the first lights.

Incidentally the key familiarly penetrated the keyhole.

Armando would open the door. He'd switch the light on.

And suddenly in the doorframe the expectant face that he constantly tried to mask but couldn't suppress would be bared. Then his bated breath would finally transform into a smile of great unburdening. That embarrassed smile of relief that he'd never suspected she noticed. That relief they had probably, with a pat on the back, advised her poor husband to conceal. But which, for his wife's guilt-ridden heart, had been daily reward for at last having given back to that man the possibility of joy and peace, sanctified by the hand of an austere priest who only allowed beings a humble joy and not the imitation of Christ.

The key turned in the lock, the shadowy and hurried figure entered, light violently flooded the room.

And right in the doorway he froze with that panting and suddenly paralyzed look as if he'd run for miles so as not to get home too late. She was going to smile. So he could at last wipe that anxious suspense off his face, which always came mingled with the childish triumph of getting home in time to find her there boring, nice and diligent, and his wife. She was going to smile so he'd once again know that there would never again be any danger of his getting home too late. She was going to smile to teach him sweetly to believe in her. It was no use advising them never to mention the subject: they didn't talk about it but had worked out a language of facial expressions in which fear and trust were conveyed, and question and answer were mutely telegraphed. She was going to smile. It was taking a while but she was going to smile.

Calm and gentle, she said:

"It's back, Armando. It's back."

As if he would never understand, his face twisted into a dubious smile. His primary task at the moment was trying to catch his breath after sprinting up the stairs, since he'd triumphantly avoided getting home late, since there she was smiling at him. As if he'd never understand.

"What's back," he finally asked in a blank tone of voice.

But, as he was trying never to understand, the man's progressively stiffening face had already understood, though not a single feature had altered. His primary task was to stall for time and concentrate on catching his breath. Which suddenly was no longer hard to do. For unexpectedly he realized in horror that both the living room and his wife were calm and unhurried. With even further misgiving, like someone who bursts into laughter after getting the joke, he nonetheless insisted on keeping his face contorted, from which he watched her warily, almost her enemy. And from which he was starting to no longer help noticing how she was sitting with her hands crossed on her lap, with the serenity of a lit-up firefly.

In her brown-eyed and innocent gaze the proud embarrassment of not having been able to resist.

"What's back," he said suddenly harsh.

"I couldn't help it," she said, and her final compassion for the man was in her voice, that final plea for forgiveness already mingled with the haughtiness of a solitude almost perfect now. I couldn't help it, she repeated surrendering to him in relief the compassion she had struggled to hold onto until he got home. "It was because of the roses," she said modestly.

As if holding still for a snapshot of that instant, he kept that same detached face, as if the photographer had wanted only his face and not his soul. He opened his mouth and for an instant his face involuntarily took on that expression of comic indifference he'd used to hide his mortification when asking his boss for a raise. The next second, he averted his eyes in shame at the indecency of his wife who, blossoming and serene, was sitting there.

But suddenly the tension fell away. His shoulders sagged, his features gave way and a great heaviness relaxed him. He looked at her older now, curious.

She was sitting there in her little housedress. He knew she'd done what she could to avoid becoming luminous and unattainable. Timidly and with respect, he was looking at her. He'd grown older, weary, curious. But he didn't have a single word to say. From the open doorway he saw his wife on the sofa without leaning back, once again alert and tranquil, as if on a train. That had already departed.

Happy Birthday
("Feliz aniversário")

THE FAMILY BEGAN ARRIVING IN WAVES. THE ONES from Olaria were all dressed up because the visit also meant an outing in Copacabana. The daughter-in-law from Olaria showed up in navy blue, glittering with "pailletés" and draping that camouflaged her ungirdled belly. Her husband didn't come for obvious reasons: he didn't want to see his siblings. But he'd sent his wife so as not to sever all ties—and she came in her best dress to show that she didn't need any of them, along with her three children: two girls with already budding breasts, infantilized in pink ruffles and starched petticoats, and the boy sheepish in his new suit and tie.

Since Zilda—the daughter with whom the birthday girl lived—had placed chairs side-by-side along the walls, as at a party where there's going to be dancing, the daughter-in-law from Olaria, after greeting the members of the household with a stony expression, plunked herself down in one of the chairs and fell silent, lips pursed, maintaining her offended stance. "I came to avoid not coming," she'd said to Zilda, and then had sat feeling offended. The two little misses in pink and the boy, sallow and with their hair neatly combed, didn't really know how to behave and stood beside their mother, impressed by her navy blue dress and the "pailletés."

Then the daughter-in-law from Ipanema came with two grandsons and the nanny. Her husband would come later. And since Zilda—the only girl among six brothers and the only one who, it had been decided years ago, had the space and time to take in the birthday girl—and since Zilda was in the kitchen with the maid putting the finishing touches on the croquettes and sandwiches, that left: the stuck-up daughter-in-law from Olaria with her anxious-hearted children by her side; the daughter-in-law from Ipanema in the opposite row of chairs pretending to deal with the baby to avoid facing her sister-in-law from Olaria; the idle, uniformed nanny, her mouth hanging open.

And at the head of the large table the birthday girl who was turning eighty-nine today.

Zilda, the lady of the house, had set the table early, covered it with colorful paper napkins and birthday-themed paper cups, scattered balloons drifting along the ceiling on some of which was written "Happy Birthday!", on others "Feliz Aniversário!". At the center she'd placed the enormous frosted cake. To move things along, she'd decorated the table right after lunch, pushed the chairs against the wall, sent the boys out to play at the neighbor's so they wouldn't mess up the table.

And, to move things along, she'd dressed the birthday girl right after lunch. Since then she'd fastened that pendant around her neck and pinned on her brooch, sprayed her with a little perfume to cover that musty smell of hers—seated her at the table. And since two o'clock the birthday girl had been sitting at the head of the long empty table, rigid in the silent room.

Occasionally aware of the colorful napkins. Looking curiously when a passing car made the odd balloon tremble. And occasionally that mute anguish: whenever she watched, fascinated and powerless, the buzzing of a fly around the cake.

Until four o'clock when the daughter-in-law from Olaria arrived followed by the one from Ipanema.

Just when the daughter-in-law from Ipanema thought she couldn't bear another second of being seated directly across from her sister-in-law from Olaria—who brimming with past offenses saw no reason to stop glaring defiantly at the daughter-in-law from Ipanema—at last José and his family arrived. And as soon as they all kissed the room started filling with people greeting each other loudly as if they'd all been waiting below for the right moment to, in the rush of being late, stride up the three flights of stairs, talking, dragging along startled children, crowding into the room—and kicking off the party.

The birthday girl's facial muscles no longer expressed her, so no one could tell whether she was in a good mood. Placed at the head was what she was. She amounted to a large, thin, powerless and dark old woman. She looked hollow.

"Eighty-nine years old, yes sir!" said José, the eldest now that Jonga had died. "Eighty-nine years old, yes ma'am!" he said rubbing his hands in public admiration and as an imperceptible signal to everyone.

Everyone broke off attentively and looked over at the birthday girl in a more official manner. Some shook their heads in awe as if she'd set a record. Each year conquered by the birthday girl was a vague step forward for the whole family. "Yes sir!" a few said smiling shyly.

"Eighty-nine years old!" echoed Manoel, who was José's business partner. "Just a little sprout!" he said joking and nervous, and everyone laughed except his wife.

The old woman showed no expression.

Some hadn't brought her a present. Others brought a soap dish, a cotton slip, a costume jewelry brooch, a little potted cactus—nothing, nothing that the lady of the house could use for herself or her children, nothing that the birthday girl herself could really use and thereby save money for the lady of the house: she put away the presents, bitter, sarcastic.

"Eighty-nine years old!" repeated Manoel nervously, looking at his wife.

The old woman showed no expression.

And so, as if everyone had received the final proof that there was no point making any effort, with a shrug as if they were there with a deaf woman, they kept the party going by themselves, eating the first ham sandwiches more as a show of enthusiasm than out of hunger, making as if they were all starving to death. The punch was served, Zilda was sweating, not a single sister-in-law was really helping, the hot grease from the croquettes gave off the smell of a picnic; and with their backs turned to the birthday girl, who couldn't eat fried food, they laughed nervously. And Cordélia? Cordélia, the youngest daughter-in-law, seated, smiling.

"No sir!" José replied with mock severity, "no shop talk today!"

"Right, right!" Manoel quickly backed down, darting a look at his wife whose ears pricked up from a distance.

"No shop talk," José boomed, "today is for Mother!"

At the head of the already messy table, the cups dirtied, only the cake intact—she was the mother. The birthday girl blinked.

And by the time the table was filthy, the mothers irritated at the racket their children were making, while the grandmothers were leaning back complacently in their chairs, that was when they turned off the useless hallway light so as to light the candle on the cake, a big candle with a small piece of paper stuck to it on which was written "89." But no one praised Zilda's idea, and she wondered anxiously if they thought she was trying to save candles—nobody recalling that nobody had contributed so much as a box of matches for the party food that she, Zilda, was serving like a slave, her feet exhausted and her heart in revolt. Then they lit the candle. And then José, the leader, sang with great gusto, galvanizing the most hesitant or surprised ones with an authoritarian stare, "come on! all together now!"—and they all suddenly joined in singing loud as soldiers. Roused by the voices, Cordélia looked on breathlessly. Since they hadn't coordinated ahead of time, some sang in Portuguese and others in English. Then they tried to correct it: and the ones who'd been singing in English switched to Portuguese, and the ones who'd been singing in Portuguese switched to singing very softly in English.

While they were singing, the birthday girl, in the glow of the lit candle, meditated as though by the fireside.

They picked the youngest great-grandchild who, propped in his encouraging mother's lap, blew out the candle in a single breath full of saliva! For an instant they applauded the unexpected power of the boy who, astonished and exultant, looked around at everyone in rapture. The lady of the house was waiting with her finger poised on the hallway switch—and turned on the light.

"Long live Mama!"

"Long live Grandma!"

"Long live Dona Anita," said the neighbor who had shown up.

"Happy Birthday!" shouted the grandchildren who studied English at the Bennett School.

A few hands were still clapping.

The birthday girl was staring at the large, dry, extinguished cake.

"Cut the cake, Grandma!" said the mother of four, "she should be the one to cut it!" she asserted uncertainly to everyone, in an intimate and scheming manner. And, since they all approved happily and curiously, she suddenly became impetuous: "cut the cake, Grandma!"

And suddenly the old woman grabbed the knife. And without hesitation, as if in hesitating for a moment she might fall over, she cut the first slice with a murderer's thrust.

"So strong," the daughter-in-law from Ipanema murmured, and it wasn't clear whether she was shocked or pleasantly surprised. She was a little horrified.

"A year ago she could still climb these stairs better than me," said Zilda bitterly.

With the first slice cut, as though the first shovelful of dirt had been dug, they all closed in with their plates in hand, elbowing each other in feigned excitement, each going after his own little shovelful.

Soon enough the slices were divided among the little plates, in a silence full of commotion. The younger children, their mouths hidden by the table and their eyes at its level, watched the distribution with mute intensity. Raisins rolled out of the cake amid dry crumbs. The anguished children saw the raisins being wasted, intently watching them drop.

And when they went over to see, wouldn't you know the birthday girl was already devouring her last bite?

And so to speak the party was over.

Cordélia looked at everyone absently, smiling.

"I already told you: no shop talk today!" José replied beaming.

"Right, right!" Manoel backed down placatingly without glancing at his wife who didn't take her eyes off him. "You're right," Manoel tried to smile and a convulsion passed rapidly over the muscles of his face.

"Today is for Mother!" José said.

At the head of the table, the tablecloth stained with Coca-Cola, the cake in ruins, she was the mother. The birthday girl blinked.

There they were milling about boisterously, laughing, her family. And she was the mother of them all. And what if she suddenly got up, as a corpse rises slowly and imposes muteness and terror upon the living, the birthday girl stiffened in her chair, sitting up taller. She was the mother of them all. And since her pendant was suffocating her, she was the mother of them all and, powerless in her chair, she despised them all. And looked at them blinking. All those children and grandchildren and great-grandchildren of hers who were no more than the flesh of her knee, she thought suddenly as if spitting. Rodrigo, her seven-year-old grandson, was the only one who was the flesh of her heart, Rodrigo, with that tough little face, virile and tousled. Where's Rodrigo? Rodrigo with the drowsy, tumescent gaze in that ardent and confused little head. That one would turn out to be a man. But, blinking, she looked at the others, the birthday girl. Oh how despicable those failed lives. How?! how could someone as strong as she have given birth to those dimwitted beings, with their slack arms and anxious faces? She, the strong one, who had married at the proper hour and time a good man whom, obediently and independently, she respected; whom she respected and who gave her children and repaid her for giving birth and honored her recovery time. The trunk was sound. But it had borne these sour and unfortunate fruits, lacking even the capacity for real joy. How could she have given birth to those frivolous, weak, self-indulgent beings? The resentment rumbled in her empty chest. A bunch of communists, that's what they were; communists. She glared at them with her old woman's ire. They looked like rats jostling each other, her family. Irrepressible, she turned her head and with unsuspected force spit on the ground.

"Mama!" cried the lady of the house, mortified. "What's going on, Mama!" she cried utterly mortified, and didn't even want to look at the others, she knew those good-for-nothings were exchanging triumphant glances as if it was up to her to make the old woman behave, and it wouldn't be long before they were claiming she didn't bathe their mother anymore, they'd never understand the sacrifice she was making. "Mama, what's going on!" she said softly, in anguish. "You've never done this before!" she added loudly so everyone would hear, she wanted to join the others' shock, when the cock crows for the third time you shall renounce your mother. But her enormous humiliation was soothed when she realized they were shaking their heads as if they agreed that the old woman was now no more than a child.

"Lately she's been spitting," she ended up confessing apologetically to everyone.

Everyone looked at the birthday girl, commiserating, respectful, in silence.

They looked like rats jostling each other, her family. The boys, though grown—probably already in their fifties, for all I know!—the boys still retained some of their handsome features. But those wives they had chosen! And the wives her grandchildren—weaker and more sour still—had chosen. All vain with slender legs, and those fake necklaces for women who when it comes down to it can't take the heat, those wimpy women who married off their sons poorly, who didn't know how to put a maid in her place, and all their ears dripping with jewelry—none, none of it real gold! Rage was suffocating her.

"Give me a glass of wine!" she said.

Silence fell suddenly, everyone with a cup frozen in their hand.

"Granny darling, won't it make you sick?" the short, plump little granddaughter ventured cautiously.

"To hell with Granny darling!" the birthday girl exploded bitterly. "The devil take you, you pack of sissies, cuckolds and whores! give me a glass of wine, Dorothy!" she ordered.

Dorothy didn't know what to do, she looked around at everyone in a comical plea for help. But, like detached and unassailable masks, suddenly not a single face showed any expression. The party interrupted, half-eaten sandwiches in their hands, some dry piece stuck in their mouths, bulging their cheeks with the worst timing. They'd all gone blind, deaf and dumb, croquettes in their hands. And they stared impassively.

Forsaken, amused, Dorothy gave her the wine: slyly just two fingertips' worth in the cup. Expressionless, at the ready, they all awaited the storm.

But not only did the birthday girl not explode at the miserable splash of wine Dorothy had given her but she didn't even touch the cup.

Her gaze was fixed, silent. As if nothing had happened.

Everyone exchanged polite glances, smiling blindly, abstractedly as if a dog had peed in the room. Stoically, the voices and laughter started back up. The daughter-in-law from Olaria, who had experienced her first moment in unison with the others just when the tragedy triumphantly seemed about to be unleashed, had to retreat alone to her severity, without even the solidarity of her three children who were now mingling traitorously with the others. From her reclusive chair, she critically appraised those shapeless dresses, without any draping, their obsession with pairing a black dress with pearls, which was anything but stylish, cheap was all it was. Eyeing from afar those meagerly buttered sandwiches. She hadn't helped herself to a thing, not a thing! She'd only had one of each, just to taste.

And so to speak, once again the party was over.

People graciously remained seated. Some with their attention turned inward, waiting for something to say. Others vacant and expectant, with amiable smiles, stomachs full of that junk that didn't nourish but got rid of hunger. The children, already out of control, shrieked rambunctiously. Some already had filthy faces; the other, younger ones, were already wet; the afternoon was fading rapidly. And Cordélia, Cordélia looked on absently, with a dazed smile, bearing her secret in solitude. What's the matter with her? someone asked with a negligent curiosity, head gesturing at her from afar, but no one answered. They turned on the remaining lights to hasten the tranquility of the night, the children were starting to bicker. But the lights were fainter than the faint tension of the afternoon. And the twilight of Copacabana, unyielding, meanwhile kept expanding and penetrating the windows like a weight.

"I have to go," one of the daughters-in-law said, disturbed, standing and brushing the crumbs off her skirt. Several others rose smiling.

The birthday girl received a cautious kiss from each of them as if her so unfamiliar skin were a trap. And, impassive, blinking, she took in those deliberately incoherent words they said to her attempting to give a final thrust of enthusiasm to something that was no more than the past: night had now fallen almost completely. The light in the room then seemed yellower and richer, the people older. The children were already hysterical.

"Does she think the cake takes the place of dinner," the old woman wondered in the depths of herself.

But no one could have guessed what she was thinking. And for those who looked at her once more from the doorway, the birthday girl was only what she appeared to be: seated at the head of the filthy table, her hand clenched on the tablecloth as though grasping a scepter, and with that muteness that was her last word. Fist clenched on the table, never again would she be only what she was thinking. Her appearance had finally surpassed her and, going beyond her, was serenely becoming gigantic. Cordélia stared at her in alarm. The mute and severe fist on the table was telling the unhappy daughter-in-law she irremediably loved perhaps for the last time: You must know. You must know. That life is short. That life is short.

Yet she didn't repeat it anymore. Because truth was a glimpse. Cordélia stared at her in terror. And, for the very last time, she never repeated it—while Rodrigo, the birthday girl's grandson, tugged at Cordélia's hand, tugged at the hand of that guilty, bewildered and desperate mother who once more looked back imploring old age to give one more sign that a woman should, in a heartrending impulse, finally cling to her last chance and live. Once more Cordélia wanted to look.

But when she looked again—the birthday girl was an old woman at the head of the table.

The glimpse had passed. And dragged onward by Rodrigo's patient and insistent hand the daughter-in-law followed him in alarm.

"Not everyone has the privilege and the honor to gather

around their mother," José cleared his throat recalling that Jonga had been the one who gave speeches.

"Their mother, sure!" his niece snickered, and the slowest cousin laughed without getting it.

"We have," Manoel said dispiritedly, no longer looking at his wife. "We have this great privilege," he said distractedly wiping his moist palms.

But that wasn't it at all, merely the distress of farewells, never knowing just what to say, José expecting from himself with perseverance and confidence the next line of the speech. Which didn't come. Which didn't come. Which didn't come. The others were waiting. How he missed Jonga at times like this—José wiped his brow with his handkerchief—how he missed Jonga at times like this! He'd also been the only one whom the old woman had always approved of and respected, and this gave Jonga so much self-assurance. And when he died, the old woman never spoke of him again, placing a wall between his death and the others. She'd forgotten him perhaps. But she hadn't forgotten that same firm and piercing gaze she'd always directed at the other children, always causing them to avert their eyes. A mother's love was hard to bear: José wiped his brow, heroic, smiling.

And suddenly the line came:

"See you next year!" José suddenly exclaimed mischievously, finding, thus, just like that, the right turn of phrase: a lucky hint! "See you next year, eh?" he repeated afraid he hadn't been understood.

He looked at her, proud of the cunning old woman who was always clever enough to live another year.

"Next year we'll meet again around the birthday cake!" her son Manoel further clarified, improving on his business partner's wit. "See you next year, Mama! and around the birthday cake!" he said in thorough explanation, right in her ear, while looking obligingly at José. And the old woman suddenly let out a weak cackle, understanding the allusion.

Then she opened her mouth and said:

"Sure."

Excited that it had gone so unexpectedly well, José shouted at her with emotion, grateful, his eyes moist:

"We'll see each other next year, Mama!"

"I'm not deaf!" said the birthday girl gruffly, affectionately.

Her children looked at each other laughing, embarrassed, happy. It had worked out.

The kids went off in good spirits, their appetites ruined. The daughter-in-law from Olaria vengefully cuffed her son, too cheerful and no longer wearing his tie. The stairs were difficult, dark, it was unbelievable to insist on living in such a cramped building that would have to be demolished any day now, and while being evicted Zilda would still cause trouble and want to push the old woman onto the daughters-in-law— reaching the last step, the guests relievedly found themselves in the cool calm of the street. It was nighttime, yes. With its first shiver.

Goodbye, see you soon, we have to get together. Stop by sometime, they said quickly. Some managed to look the others in the eye with unflinching cordiality. Some buttoned up their children's coats, looking at the sky for some hint of the weather. Everyone obscurely feeling that when saying goodbye you could maybe, now without the threat of commitment, be nice and say that extra word—which word? they didn't know exactly, and looked at each other smiling, mute. It was an instant that was begging to come alive. But that was dead. They started going their separate ways, walking with their backs slightly turned, unsure how to break away from their relatives without being abrupt.

"See you next year!" José repeated the lucky hint, waving with effusive vigor, his thinning, white hair fluttering. He really was fat, they thought, he'd better watch his heart. "See you next year!" José boomed, eloquent and grand, and his height seemed it might crumble. But those already a ways off didn't know whether to laugh loudly for him to hear or if it was enough to smile even in the darkness. More than a few thought that luckily the hint contained more than just a joke and that not until next year would they have to gather around the birthday cake; while others, already farther off in the darkness of the street, wondered whether the old woman would hang on for another year of Zilda's nerves and impatience, but honestly there was nothing they could do about it. "Ninety years old at the very least," thought the daughter-in-law from Ipanema melancholically. "To make it to a nice, round age," she thought dreamily.

Meanwhile, up above, atop the stairs and contingencies, the birthday girl was seated at the head of the table, erect, definitive, greater than herself. What if there's no dinner tonight, she mused. Death was her mystery.

The Smallest Woman in the World
("A menor mulher do mundo")

IN THE DEPTHS OF EQUATORIAL AFRICA THE FRENCH explorer Marcel Pretre, hunter and man of the world, came upon a pygmy tribe of surprising smallness. He was all the more surprised, then, when informed that an even smaller people existed beyond forests and distances. So deeper still he plunged.

In the Central Congo he indeed discovered the smallest pygmies in the world. And—like a box within a box, within a box—among the smallest pygmies in the world was the smallest of the smallest pygmies in the world, obeying perhaps the need Nature sometimes has to outdo herself.

Amid mosquitoes and trees warm with moisture, amid the rich leaves of the laziest green, Marcel Pretre came face-to-face with a woman who stood eighteen inches tall, full-grown, black, silent. "Dark as a monkey," he would inform the press, and that she lived in the top of a tree with her little consort. In the tepid, wild mists, which swell the fruits early and make them taste almost intolerably sweet, she was pregnant.

There she stood, then, the smallest woman in the world. For an instant, in the drone of the heat, it was as if the Frenchman had unexpectedly arrived at the last conclusion. Undoubtedly, it was only because he wasn't insane, that his soul neither fainted nor lost control. Sensing an immediate need for order, and to give a name to whatever exists, he dubbed her Little Flower. And, in order to classify her among the recognizable realities, he quickly set about collecting data on her.

Her race is gradually being exterminated. Few human examples remain of this species which, if not for the cunning danger of Africa, would be a dispersed people. Aside from disease, infectious vapors from the waters, insufficient food and roving beasts, the greatest risk facing the scant Likoualas are the savage Bantus, a threat that surrounds them in the silent air as on the morning of battle. The Bantus hunt them with nets, as they do monkeys. And eat them. Just like that: they hunt them with nets and Eat them. That tiny race of people, always retreating and retreating, eventually took up residence in the heart of Africa, where the lucky explorer would discover them. For strategic defense, they live in the tallest trees. From which the women descend to cook corn, grind cassava and gather vegetables; the men, to hunt. When a child is born, he is granted his freedom almost immediately. It's true that often the child won't enjoy this freedom for very long among wild beasts. But then it's true that, at the very least, no one will lament that, for so short a life, the labor was long. For even the language the child learns is short and simple, strictly essential. The Likoualas use few names, referring to things with gestures and animal sounds. In terms of spiritual advancement, they have a drum. While they dance to the sound of the drum, a little male stands guard against the Bantus, who will come from no one knows where.

It was, therefore, thus, that the explorer discovered, standing there at his feet, the smallest human thing in existence.

His heart beat because no emerald is as rare. Neither are the teachings of the sages of India as rare. Neither has the richest man in the world ever laid eyes on so much strange grace. Right there was a woman the gluttony of the most exquisite dream could never have imagined. That was when the explorer declared, shyly and with a delicacy of feeling of which his wife would never have judged him capable:

"You are Little Flower."

At that moment Little Flower scratched herself where a person doesn't scratch. The explorer—as if receiving the highest prize for chastity to which a man, who had always been so idealistic, dared aspire—the explorer, seasoned as he was, averted his eyes.

Little Flower's photograph was published in the color supplement of the Sunday papers, where she fit life-size. Wrapped in a cloth, with her belly far along. Her nose flat, her face black, eyes sunken, feet splayed. She resembled a dog.

That Sunday, in an apartment, a woman, seeing Little Flower's picture in the open newspaper, didn't want to look a second time "because it pains me so."

In another apartment a lady felt such perverse tenderness for the African woman's smallness that—prevention being better than cure—no one should ever leave Little Flower alone with the lady's tenderness. Who knows to what darkness of love affection can lead. The lady was disturbed for a day, one might say seized with longing. Besides it was spring, a dangerous benevolence was in the air.

In another house a five-year-old girl, seeing the picture and hearing the commentary, became alarmed. In that household of adults, this girl had up till now been the smallest of human beings. And, if that was the source of the best caresses, it was also the source of this first fear of love's tyranny. Little Flower's existence led the girl to feel—with a vagueness that only years and years later, for very different reasons, would solidify into thought—led her to feel, in a first flash of wisdom, that "misfortune has no limit."

In another house, amid the rite of spring, the young bride-to-be experienced an ecstasy of compassion:

"Mama, look at her little picture, poor little thing! just look how sad she is!"

"But," said the mother, firm and defeated and proud, "but it's the sadness of an animal, not human sadness."

"Oh! Mama," said the girl discouraged.

It was in another house that a clever boy had a clever idea:

"Mama, what if I put that little African lady on Paulinho's bed while he's sleeping? when he wakes up, he'll be so scared, right! he'll scream, when he sees her sitting on the bed! And then we could play so much with her! we could make her our toy, right!"

His mother was at that moment curling her hair in front of the bathroom mirror, and she recalled something a cook had told her about her time at the orphanage. Having no dolls to play with, and maternity already pulsating terribly in the hearts of those orphans, the sly little girls had concealed another girl's death from the nun. They hid the corpse in a wardrobe until the nun left, and played with the dead girl, giving her baths and little snacks, punishing her just so they could kiss her afterward, consoling her. This is what the mother recalled in the bathroom, and she lowered her pendulous hands, full of hairpins. And considered the cruel necessity of loving. She considered the malignity of our desire to be happy. Considered the ferocity with which we want to play. And how many times we will kill out of love. Then she looked at her clever son as if looking at a dangerous stranger. And she felt horror at her own soul that, more than her body, had engendered that being fit for life and happiness. That is how she looked, with careful attention and an uncomfortable pride, at that boy already missing his two front teeth, evolution, evolution in action, a tooth falling out to make way for one better for biting. "I'm going to buy him a new suit," she decided looking at him deep in thought. Obstinately she dressed her gap-toothed son in nice clothes, obstinately wanting him to be squeaky clean, as if cleanliness would emphasize a calming superficiality, obstinately perfecting the courteous side of beauty. Obstinately distancing herself, and distancing him, from something that ought to be "dark like a monkey." Then, looking in the bathroom mirror, the mother made a deliberately refined and polite smile, placing, between that face of hers with its abstract lines and Little Flower's crude face, the insurmountable distance of millennia. But, after years of practice, she knew this would be one of those Sundays on which she'd have to conceal from herself the anxiety, the dream, and millennia lost.

In another house, beside a wall, they were engaged in the excited task of measuring Little Flower's eighteen inches with a ruler. And that was where, delighted, they gasped in shock: she was even smaller than the keenest imagination could conceive. In each family member's heart arose, nostalgic, the desire to have that tiny and indomitable thing for himself, that thing spared from being eaten, that permanent source of charity. The family's eager soul wanted to devote itself. And, really, who hasn't ever wished to possess a human being for one's very own? Which, to be sure, wouldn't always be convenient, there are times when you don't want to have feelings:

"I bet if she lived here, it would lead to fighting," said the father seated in his armchair, definitively turning the page of his newspaper. "In this house everything leads to fighting."

"There you go again, José, always pessimistic," said the mother.

"Mama, have you thought about how tiny her little baby would be?" the eldest daughter, age thirteen, said ardently.

The father stirred behind his newspaper.

"It must be the smallest black baby in the world," replied the mother, oozing with pleasure. "Just imagine her serving dinner here at home! and with that enormous little belly!"

"Enough of this chatter!" the father growled.

"But you must admit," said the mother unexpectedly offended, "that we're talking about a rare thing. You're the one being insensitive."

And the rare thing herself?

Meanwhile, in Africa, the rare thing herself held in her heart—who knows, maybe it was black too, since a Nature that's erred once can no longer be trusted—meanwhile the rare thing herself harbored in her heart something rarer still, like the secret of the secret itself: a tiny child. Methodically the explorer peered closely at the little belly of the smallest full-grown human being. In that instant the explorer, for the first time since he'd met her, instead of feeling curiosity or exaltation or triumph or the scientific spirit, the explorer felt distress.

Because the smallest woman in the world was laughing.

She was laughing, warm, warm. Little Flower was delighting in life. The rare thing herself was having the ineffable sensation of not yet having been eaten. Not having been eaten was something that, at other times, gave her the agile impulse to leap from branch to branch. But, in this moment of tranquility, amidst the dense leaves of the Central Congo, she wasn't putting that impulse into action—and the impulse had become concentrated entirely in the smallness of the rare thing herself. And so she was laughing. It was a laugh that only one who doesn't speak, laughs. That laugh, the embarrassed explorer couldn't manage to classify. And she kept enjoying her own soft laughter, she who wasn't being devoured. Not being devoured is the most perfect of feelings. Not being devoured is the secret goal of an entire life. So long as she wasn't being eaten, her bestial laughter was as delicate as joy is delicate. The explorer was confounded.

Second of all, if the rare thing herself was laughing, it was because, within her smallness, a great darkness had sprung into motion.

It was that the rare thing herself felt her breast warmed with what might be called Love. She loved that yellow explorer. If she knew how to speak and told him she loved him, he'd puff up with vanity. Vanity that would shrivel when she added that she also loved the explorer's ring very much and that she loved the explorer's boots very much. And when he deflated in disappointment, Little Flower wouldn't understand why. For, not in the slightest, would her love for the explorer—one might even say her "profound love," because, having no other resources, she was reduced to profundity—for not in the slightest would her profound love for the explorer be devalued by the fact that she also loved his boots. There's an old mistake about the word love, and, if many children have been born of this mistake, countless others have missed their only instant of being born merely due to a susceptibility that demands you be mine, mine! that you like me, and not my money. But in the humidity of the forest there are no such cruel refinements, and love is not being eaten, love is thinking a boot is pretty, love is liking that rare color of a man who isn't black, love is laughing with the love of a ring that sparkles. Little Flower blinked with love, and laughed warm, tiny, pregnant, warm.

The explorer tried to smile back at her, without knowing exactly to what abyss his smile responded, and then got flustered as only a big man gets flustered. He pretended to adjust his explorer helmet, blushing bashfully. He turned a lovely color, his own, a greenish pink, like that of a lime at dawn. He must have been sour.

It was probably while adjusting his symbolic helmet that the explorer pulled himself together, severely regained the discipline of work, and recommenced taking notes. He'd learned some of the few words spoken by the tribe, and how to interpret their signals. He could already ask questions.

Little Flower answered "yes." That it was very good to have a tree to live in, her own, her very own. For—and this she didn't say, but her eyes went so dark that they said it—for it is good to possess, good to possess, good to possess. The explorer blinked several times.

Marcel Pretre had several difficult moments with himself. But at least he kept busy by taking lots of notes. Those who didn't take notes had to deal with themselves as best they could:

"Because look,"—suddenly declared an old woman shutting the newspaper decisively—"because look, all I'll say is this: God knows what He's doing."

Family Ties
("Os laços de família")

THE WOMAN AND HER MOTHER FINALLY SQUEEZED into the taxi that was taking them to the station. The mother kept counting and recounting the two suitcases trying to convince herself that both were in the car. The daughter, with her dark eyes, whose slightly cross-eyed quality gave them a constant glimmer of derision and detachment—watched.

"I haven't forgotten anything?" the mother was asking for the third time.

"No, no, you haven't forgotten anything," the daughter answered in amusement, patiently.

That somewhat comic scene between her mother and her husband still lingered in her mind, when it came time to say goodbye. For the entire two weeks of the old woman's visit, the two could barely stand each other; their good-mornings and good-afternoons constantly struck a note of cautious tact that made her want to laugh. But right when saying goodbye, before getting into the taxi, her mother had transformed into a model mother-in-law and her husband had become the good son-in-law. "Forgive any misspoken words," the old lady had said, and Catarina, taking some joy in it, had seen Antônio fumble with the suitcases in his hands, stammering—flustered at being the good son-in-law. "If I laugh, they'll think I'm mad," Catarina had thought, frowning. "Whoever marries off a son loses a son, whoever marries off a daughter gains a son," her mother had added, and Antônio took advantage of having the flu to cough. Catarina, standing there, had mischievously observed her husband whose self-assurance gave way to a diminutive, dark-haired man, forced to be a son to that tiny graying woman ... Just then her urge to laugh intensified. Luckily she never actually had to laugh whenever she got the urge: her eyes took on a sly, restrained look, went even more cross-eyed—and her laughter came out through her eyes. Being able to laugh always hurt a little. But she couldn't help it: ever since she was little she'd laughed through her eyes, she'd always been cross-eyed.

"I'll say it again, that boy is too skinny," her mother declared while bracing herself against the jolting of the car. And though Antônio wasn't there, she adopted the same combative, accusatory tone she used with him. So much that one night Antônio had lost his temper: "It's not my fault, Severina!" He called his mother-in-law Severina, since before the wedding he'd envisioned them as a modern mother- and son-in-law. Starting from her mother's first visit to the couple, the word Severina had turned leaden in her husband's mouth, and so, now, the fact that he used her first name hadn't stopped ... —Catarina would look at them and laugh.

"The boy's always been skinny, Mama," she replied.

The taxi drove on monotonously.

"Skinny and anxious," added the old lady decisively.

"Skinny and anxious," Catarina agreed patiently.

He was an anxious, distracted boy. During his grandmother's visit he'd become even more remote, slept poorly, was upset by the old woman's excessive affection and loving pinches. Antônio, who'd never been particularly worried about his son's sensitivity, had begun dropping hints to his mother-in-law, "to protect a child" ...

"I haven't forgotten anything ..." her mother started up again, when the car suddenly braked, launching them into each other and sending their suitcases flying. Oh! oh!, shouted her mother as if faced with some irremediable disaster, "oh!" she said shaking her head in surprise, suddenly older and pitiable. And Catarina?

Catarina looked at her mother, and mother looked at daughter, and had some disaster also befallen Catarina? her eyes blinked in surprise, she quickly righted the suitcases and her purse, trying to remedy the catastrophe as fast as possible. Because something had indeed happened, there was no point hiding it: Catarina had been launched into Severina, into a long forgotten bodily intimacy, going back to the age when one has a father and mother. Though they'd never really hugged or kissed. With her father, yes, Catarina had always been more of a friend. Whenever her mother would fill their plates making them overeat, the two would wink at each other conspiratorially and her mother never even noticed. But after colliding in the taxi and after regaining their composure, they had nothing to talk about—why weren't they already at the station?

"I haven't forgotten anything," her mother asked in a resigned voice.

Catarina no longer wished to look at her or answer.

"Take your gloves!" she said as she picked them up off the ground.

"Oh! oh! my gloves!" her mother exclaimed, flustered.

They only really looked at each other once the suitcases were deposited on the train, after they'd exchanged kisses: her mother's head appeared at the window.

Catarina then saw that her mother had aged and that her eyes were glistening.

The train wasn't leaving and they waited with nothing to say. The mother pulled a mirror from her purse and studied herself in her new hat, bought at the same milliner's where her daughter went. She gazed at herself while making an excessively severe expression that didn't lack in self-admiration. Her daughter watched in amusement. No one but me can love you, thought the woman laughing through her eyes; and the weight of that responsibility left the taste of blood in her mouth. As if "mother and daughter" were life and abhorrence. No, you couldn't say she loved her mother. Her mother pained her, that was all. The old woman had slipped the mirror back into her purse, and was smiling steadily at her. Her worn and still quite clever face looked like it was struggling to make a certain impression on the people around her, in which her hat played a role. The station bell suddenly rang, there was a general movement of anxiousness, several people broke into a run thinking the train was already leaving: Mama! the woman said. Catarina! the old woman said. They gaped at each other, the suitcase on a porter's head blocked their view and a young man rushing past grabbed Catarina's arm in passing, jerking the collar of her dress off-kilter. When they could see each other again, Catarina was on the verge of asking if she'd forgotten anything...

"... I haven't forgotten anything?" her mother asked.

Catarina also had the feeling they'd forgotten something,

and they looked at each other at a loss—for if they really had forgotten something, it was too late now. A woman dragged a child along, the child wailed, the station bell resounded again … Mama, said the woman. What was it they'd forgotten to say to each other? and now it was too late. It struck her that one day they should have said something like: "I am your mother, Catarina." And she should have answered: "And I am your daughter."

"Don't sit in the draft!" Catarina called.

"Come now, girl, I'm not a child," said her mother, never taking her attention off her own appearance. Her freckled hand, slightly tremulous, was delicately arranging the brim of her hat and Catarina suddenly wanted to ask whether she'd been happy with her father:

"Give my best to Auntie!" she shouted.

"Yes, of course!"

"Mama," said Catarina because a lengthy whistle was heard and the wheels were already turning amid the smoke.

"Catarina!" the old woman called, her mouth open and her eyes astonished, and at the first lurch her daughter saw her raise her hands to her hat: it had fallen over her nose, covering everything but her new dentures. The train was already moving and Catarina waved. Her mother's face disappeared for an instant and immediately reappeared hatless, her loosened bun spilling in white locks over her shoulders like the hair of a maiden—her face was downcast and unsmiling, perhaps no longer even seeing her daughter in the distance.

Amid the smoke Catarina began heading back, frowning, with that mischievous look of the cross-eyed. Without her mother's company, she had regained her firm stride: it was easier alone. A few men looked at her, she was sweet, a little heavyset. She walked serenely, dressed in a modern style, her short hair dyed "mahogany." And things had worked out in such a way that painful love seemed like happiness to her—everything around her was so alive and tender, the dirty street, the old trams, orange peels—strength flowed back and forth through her heart in weighty abundance. She was very pretty just then, so elegant; in step with her time and the city where she'd been born as if she had chosen it. In her cross-eyed look anyone could sense the enjoyment this woman took in the things of the world. She stared at other people boldly, trying to fasten onto those mutable figures her pleasure that was still damp with tears for her mother. She veered out of the way of oncoming cars, managed to sidestep the line for the bus, glancing around ironically; nothing could stop this little woman whose hips swayed as she walked from climbing one more mysterious step in her days.

The elevator hummed in the beachfront heat. She opened the door to her apartment while using her other hand to free herself of her little hat; she seemed poised to reap the largess of the whole world, the path opened by the mother who was burning in her chest. Antônio barely looked up from his book. Saturday afternoon had always been "his," and, as soon as Severina had left, he gladly reclaimed it, seated at his desk.

"Did 'she' leave?"

"Yes she did," answered Catarina while pushing open the door to her son's room. Ah, yes, there was the boy, she thought in sudden relief. Her son. Skinny and anxious. Ever since he could walk he'd been steady on his feet; but nearing the age of four he still spoke as if he didn't know what verbs were: he'd confirm things coldly, not linking them. There he sat fiddling with his wet towel, exact and remote. The woman felt a pleasant warmth and would have liked to capture the boy forever in that moment; she pulled the towel from his hands disapprovingly: that boy! But the boy gazed indifferently into the air, communicating with himself. He was always distracted. No one had ever really managed to hold his attention. His mother shook out the towel and her body blocked the room from his view: "Mama," said the boy. Catarina spun around. It was the first time he'd said "Mama" in that tone of voice and without asking for anything. It had been more than a confirmation: Mama! The woman kept shaking the towel violently and wondered if there was anyone she could tell what happened, but she couldn't think of anyone who'd understand what she couldn't explain. She smoothed the towel vigorously before hanging it to dry. Maybe she could explain, if she changed the way it happened. She'd explain that her son had said: "Mama, who is God." No, maybe: "Mama, boy wants God." Maybe. The truth would only fit into symbols, they'd only accept it through symbols. Her eyes smiling at her necessary lie, and above all at her own foolishness, fleeing from Severina, the woman unexpectedly laughed aloud at the boy, not just with her eyes: her whole body burst into laughter, a burst casing, and a harshness emerging as hoarseness. Ugly, the boy then said peering at her.

"Let's go for a walk!" she replied blushing and taking him by the hand.

She passed through the living room, informing her husband without breaking stride: "We're going out!" and slammed the apartment door.

Antônio hardly had time to look up from his book—and in surprise saw that the living room was already empty. Catarina! he called, but he could already hear the sound of the descending elevator. Where did they go? he wondered nervously, coughing and blowing his nose. Because Saturday was his, but he wanted his wife and his son at home while he enjoyed his Saturday. Catarina! he called irritably though he knew she could no longer hear him. He got up, went to the window and a second later spotted his wife and son on the sidewalk.

The pair had stopped, the woman perhaps deciding which way to go. And suddenly marching off.

Why was she walking so briskly, holding the child's hand? through the window he saw his wife gripping the child's hand tightly and walking swiftly, her eyes staring straight ahead; and, even without seeing it, the man could tell that her jaw was set. The child, with who-knew-what obscure comprehension, was also staring straight ahead, startled and unsuspecting. Seen from above, the two figures lost their familiar perspective, seemingly flattened to the ground and darkened against the light of the sea. The child's hair was fluttering ...

The husband repeated his question to himself, which, though cloaked in the innocence of an everyday expression, worried him: where are they going? He nervously watched his wife lead the child and feared that just now when both were beyond his reach she would transmit to their son ... but what exactly? "Catarina," he thought, "Catarina, this child is still innocent!" Just when does a mother, holding a child tight, impart to him this prison of love that would forever fall heavily on the future man. Later on her son, a man now, alone, would stand before this very window, drumming his fingers against this windowpane; trapped. Forced to answer to a dead person. Who could ever know just when a mother passes this legacy to her son. And with what somber pleasure. Mother and son now understanding each other inside the shared mystery. Afterward no one would know on what black roots a man's freedom is nourished. "Catarina," he thought enraged, "that child is innocent!" Yet they'd disappeared somewhere along the beach. The shared mystery.

"But what about me? what about me?" he asked fearfully. They had gone off alone. And he had stayed behind. "With his Saturday." And his flu. In that tidy apartment, where "everything ran smoothly." What if his wife was fleeing with their son from that living room with its well-adjusted light, from the tasteful furniture, the curtains and the paintings? that was what he'd given her. An engineer's apartment. And he knew that if his wife enjoyed the situation of having a youthful husband with a promising future—she also disparaged it, with those deceitful eyes, fleeing with their anxious, skinny son. The man got worried. Since he couldn't provide her with anything but: more success. And since he knew that she'd help him achieve it and would hate whatever they accomplished. That was how this calm, thirty-two-year-old woman was, who never really spoke, as if she'd been alive forever. Their relationship was so peaceful. Sometimes he tried to humiliate her, he'd barge into their bedroom while she was changing because he knew she detested being seen naked. Why did he need to humiliate her? yet he was well aware that she would only ever belong to a man as long as she had her pride. But he had grown used to this way of making her feminine: he'd humiliate her with tenderness, and soon enough she'd smile—without resentment? Maybe this had given rise to the peaceful nature of their relationship, and those muted conversations that created a homey environment for their child. Or would he sometimes get irritable? Sometimes the boy would get irritable, stomping his feet, screaming from nightmares. What had this vibrant little creature been born from, if not from all that he and his wife had cut from their everyday life. They lived so peacefully that, if they brushed up against a moment of joy, they'd exchange rapid, almost ironic, glances, and both would say with their eyes: let's not waste it, let's not use it up frivolously. As if they'd been alive forever.

But he had spotted her from the window, seen her striding swiftly holding hands with their son, and said to himself: she's savoring a moment of joy — alone. He had felt frustrated because for a while now he hadn't been able to live unless with her. And she still managed to savor her moments — alone. For example, what had his wife been up to on the way from the train to the apartment? not that he had any suspicions but he felt uneasy.

The last light of the afternoon was heavy and beat down solemnly on the objects. The dry sands crackled. The whole day had been under this threat of radiating. Which just then, without exploding, nonetheless, grew increasingly deafening and droned on in the building's ceaseless elevator. Whenever Catarina returned they'd have dinner while swatting at the moths. The boy would cry out after first falling asleep, Catarina would interrupt dinner for a moment … and wouldn't the elevator let up for even a second?! No, the elevator wouldn't let up for a second.

"After dinner we'll go to the movies," the man decided. Because after the movies it would be night at last, and this day would shatter with the waves on the crags of Arpoador.

Mystery in São Cristóvão
("Mistério em São Cristóvão")

ONE MAY EVENING — THE HYACINTHS RIGID AGAINST
the windowpane—the dining room in a home was illuminated
and tranquil.

Around the table, frozen for an instant, sat the father, the
mother, the grandmother, three children and a skinny girl of
nineteen. The perfumed night air of São Cristóvão wasn't dangerous, but the way the people banded together inside their
home made anything beyond the family circle hazardous on a
cool May evening. There was nothing special about the gath-
ering: they had just finished dinner and were chatting around
the table, mosquitoes circling the light. What made the scene
particularly sumptuous, and each person's face so blooming,
was that after so many years this family's progress had at last
become nearly palpable: for one May evening, after dinner,
just look at how the children have been going to school every
day, the father keeps up his business, the mother has worked
throughout years of childbirth and in the home, the girl is finding her balance in the delicateness of her age, and the grandmother has attained a certain status. Without realizing this,
the family gazed happily around the room, watching over that
rare moment in May and its abundance.

Afterward they each went to their rooms. The old woman stretched out groaning benevolently. The father and mother, after locking up, lay down deep in thought and fell asleep. The three children, choosing the most awkward positions, fell asleep in three beds as if on three trapezes. The girl, in her cotton nightgown, opened her bedroom window and breathed in the whole garden with dissatisfaction and happiness. Unsettled by the fragrant humidity, she lay down promising herself a brand new outlook for the next day that would shake up the hyacinths and make the fruits tremble on their branches—in the midst of her meditation she fell asleep.

Hours passed. And when the silence was twinkling in the fireflies—the children suspended in sleep, the grandmother mulling over a difficult dream, the parents worn out, the girl asleep in the midst of her meditation—a house on the corner opened and from it emerged three masked individuals.

One was tall and had on the head of a rooster. Another was fat and had dressed as a bull. And the third, who was younger, for lack of a better idea, had disguised himself as a lord from olden times and put on a devil mask, through which his innocent eyes showed. The masked trio crossed the street in silence.

When they passed the family's darkened home, the one going as a rooster and who came up with nearly all the group's ideas, stopped and said:

"Look what we have here."

His comrades, made patient by the torture of their masks, looked and saw a house and a garden. Feeling elegant and miserable, they waited resignedly for him to finish his thought. Finally the rooster added:

"We could go pick hyacinths."

The other two didn't reply. They'd taken advantage of the delay to examine themselves despondently and try to find a way to breathe more easily inside their masks.

"A hyacinth for each of us to pin on our costumes," the rooster concluded.

The bull got riled up at the idea of yet another decoration to have to protect at the party. But, after a moment in which the three seemed to think deeply about the decision, without actually thinking about anything at all—the rooster went ahead, shimmied over the railing and set foot on the forbidden land of the garden. The bull followed with some difficulty. The third, despite some hesitation, in a single bound found himself right in the middle of the hyacinths, with a dull thud that stopped the trio dead in their tracks: holding their breath, the rooster, the bull and the devil lord peered into the darkness. But the house went on among shadows and frogs. And, in the perfume-choked garden, the hyacinths trembled unaffected.

Then the rooster pushed ahead. He could have picked the hyacinth right by his hand. The bigger ones, however, rising near a window—tall, stiff, fragile—shimmered calling out to him. The rooster headed toward them on tiptoe, and the bull and the lord went along. The silence was watching them.

Yet no sooner had he broken the largest hyacinth's stalk than the rooster stopped cold. The other two stopped with a sigh that plunged them into sleep.

From behind the dark glass of the window a white face was staring at them.

The rooster had frozen in the act of breaking off the hyacinth. The bull had halted with his hands still raised. The lord, bloodless under his mask, had regressed back to childhood and its terror. The face behind the window stared.

None of the four would ever know who was punishing whom. The hyacinths ever whiter in the darkness. Paralyzed, they peered at each other.

The simple approach of four masks on that May evening seemed to have reverberated through hollow recesses, and others, and still others that, if not for that instant in the garden, would forever remain within this perfume in the air and within the immanence of four natures that fate had singled out, designating time and place—the same precise fate of a falling star. These four, coming from reality, had fallen into the possibilities afoot on a May evening in São Cristóvão. Every moist plant, every pebble, the croaking frogs, were taking advantage of the silent confusion to better position themselves— everything in the dark was mute approach. Having fallen into the ambush, they looked at each other in terror: the nature of things had been cast into relief and the four figures peered at each other with outstretched wings. A rooster, a bull, the devil and a girl's face had unleashed the wonder of the garden … That was when the huge May moon appeared.

It was a stroke of danger for the four visages. So risky that, without a sound, four mute visions retreated without taking their eyes off each other, fearing that the moment they no longer held each other's gaze remote new territories would be ravaged, and that, after the silent collapse, only the hyacinths would remain—masters of the garden's treasure. No specter saw any other vanish because all withdrew at the same time, lingeringly, on tiptoe. No sooner, however, had the magic circle of four been broken, freed from the mutual surveillance, than the constellation broke apart in terror: three shadowy forms sprang like cats over the garden railing, and another, bristling and enlarged, backed up to the threshold of a doorway, from which, with a scream, it broke into a run.

The three masked gentlemen who, thanks to the rooster's disastrous idea, had been planning to surprise everyone at a dance happening such a long time after Carnival, were a big hit at the party already in full swing. The music broke off and those still intertwined on the dance floor saw, amid laughter, the three breathless, masked figures lurking like vagrants in the doorway. Finally, after several tries, the revelers had to abandon their wish to crown them kings of the party because, fearful, the three refused to split up: a tall one, a fat one and a young one, a fat one, a young one and a tall one, imbalance and union, their faces speechless under three masks that swung about on their own.

Meanwhile, all the lights had come on in the hyacinth house. The girl was sitting in the living room. The grandmother, her white hair braided, held the glass of water, the mother smoothed the daughter's dark hair, while the father searched the entire house. The girl couldn't explain a thing: she seemed to have said it all in her scream. Her face had clearly become smaller—the entire painstaking construction of her age had come undone, she was a little girl once more. But in her visage rejuvenated by more than one phase, there had appeared, to the family's horror, a white hair among those framing her face. Since she kept looking toward the window, they left her sitting there to rest, and, candlesticks in hand, shivering with cold in their nightgowns, set off on an expedition through the garden.

Soon the candles spread out dancing through the darkness. Ivy shrank from the sudden light, illuminated frogs hopped between feet, fruits were gilded for an instant among the leaves. The garden, roused from dreaming, sometimes grew larger sometimes winked out; somnambulant butterflies fluttered past. Finally the old woman, keen expert on the flower beds, pointed out the only visible sign in the elusive garden: the hyacinth still alive on its broken stalk … So it was true: something had happened. They returned, turned all the lights on in the house and spent the rest of the night in wait.

Only the three children slept more soundly still.

The girl gradually recovered her true age. She was the only one not constantly peering around. But the others, who hadn't seen a thing, grew watchful and uneasy. And since progress in that family was the fragile product of many precautions and a handful of lies, everything came undone and had to be remade almost from scratch: the grandmother once again quick to take offense, the father and mother fatigued, the children intolerable, the entire household seeming to hope that once more the breeze of plenty would blow one night after dinner. Which just might happen some other May evening.

The Buffalo
("O búfalo")

BUT IT WAS SPRING. EVEN THE LION LICKED THE LION-
ess's smooth forehead. Both animals blond. The woman averted
her eyes from the cage, where the hot smell alone recalled the
carnage she'd come looking for at the Zoological Garden. Then
the lion paced calmly, mane flowing, and the lioness slowly re-
composed the head of a sphinx upon her outstretched paws.
"But this is love, it's love again," railed the woman trying to locate her own hatred but it was spring and two lions had been in
love. Fists in her coat pockets, she looked around, surrounded
by the cages, caged by the shut cages. She kept walking. Her
eyes were so focused on searching that her vision sometimes
darkened into a kind of sleep, and then she'd recompose herself
as in the coolness of a pit.

But the giraffe was a virgin with freshly shorn braids. With
the mindless innocence of large and nimble and guiltless
things. The woman in the brown coat averted her eyes, feeling
sick, sick. Unable—in front of the perching aerial giraffe, in
front of that silent wingless bird—unable to locate inside herself the spot where her sickness was the worst, the sickest spot,
the spot of hatred, she who had gone to the Zoological Garden
to get sick. But not in front of the giraffe that was more land-

scape than being. Not in front of that flesh that had become distracted in its height and remoteness, the nearly verdant giraffe. She was searching for other animals, trying to learn from them how to hate. The hippopotamus, the moist hippopotamus. That plump roll of flesh, rounded and mute flesh awaiting some other plump and mute flesh. No. For there was such humble love in remaining just flesh, such sweet martyrdom in not knowing how to think.

But it was spring, and, tightening the fist in her coat pocket, she'd kill those monkeys levitating in their cage, monkeys happy as weeds, monkeys leaping about gently, the female monkey with her resigned, loving gaze, and the other female suckling her young. She'd kill them with fifteen dry bullets: the woman's teeth clenched until her jaw ached. The nakedness of the monkeys. The world that saw no danger in being naked. She'd kill the nakedness of the monkeys. One monkey stared back at her as he gripped the bars, his emaciated arms outstretched in a crucifix, his bare chest exposed without pride. But she wouldn't aim at his chest, she'd shoot the monkey between the eyes, she'd shoot between those eyes that were staring at her without blinking. Suddenly the woman averted her face: because the monkey's pupils were covered with a gelatinous white veil, in his eyes the sweetness of sickness, he was an old monkey—the woman averted her face, trapping between her teeth a feeling she hadn't come looking for, she quickened her step, even so, turned her head in alarm back toward the monkey with its arms outstretched: he kept staring straight ahead. "Oh no, not this," she thought. And as she fled, she said: "God, teach me only how to hate."

"I hate you," she said to a man whose only crime was not loving her. "I hate you," she said in a rush. But she didn't even know how you were supposed to do it. How did you dig in the earth until locating that black water, how did you open a passage through the hard earth and never reach yourself? She roamed the zoo amid mothers and children. But the elephant withstood his own weight. That whole elephant endowed with the capacity to crush with a mere foot. But he didn't crush anything. That power that nevertheless would tamely let itself be led to a circus, a children's elephant. And his eyes, with an old man's benevolence, trapped inside that hulking, inherited flesh. The oriental elephant. And the oriental spring too, and everything being born, everything flowing downstream.

The woman then tried the camel. The camel in rags, humpbacked, chewing at himself, absorbed in the process of getting to know his food. She felt weak and tired, she'd hardly eaten in two days. The camel's large, dusty eyelashes above eyes dedicated to the patience of an internal craft. Patience, patience, patience, was all she was finding in this windblown spring. Tears filled the woman's eyes, tears that didn't spill over, trapped inside the patience of her inherited flesh. The camel's dusty odor was all that arose from this encounter she had come for: for dry hatred, not for tears. She approached the bars of the pen, inhaled the dust of that old carpet where ashen blood flowed, sought its impure tepidness, pleasure ran down her back into the distress, but still not the distress she'd come looking for. In her stomach the urge to kill convulsed in hunger pangs. But not the camel in ragged burlap. "Dear God, who shall be my mate in this world?"

So she went alone to have her violence. In the zoo's small amusement park she waited meditatively in the line of lovers for her turn on the roller coaster.

And there she was sitting now, quiet in her brown coat. Her seat stopped for now, the roller-coaster machinery stopped for now. Separate from everyone in her seat, she looked like she was sitting in a Church. Her lowered eyes saw the ground between the tracks. The ground where simply out of love—love, love, not love!—where out of pure love weeds sprouted between the tracks in a light green so dizzying that she had to avert her eyes in tormented temptation. The breeze made the hair rise on the back of her neck, she shivered refusing it, in temptation refusing, it was always so much easier to love.

But all of a sudden came that lurch of the guts, that halting of a heart caught by surprise in midair, that fright, the triumphant fury with which her seat hurtled her into the nothing and immediately swept her up like a rag doll, skirts flying, the deep resentment with which she became mechanical, her body automatically joyful—the girlfriends' shrieks!—her gaze wounded by that great surprise, that offense, "they were having their way with her," that great offense—the girlfriends' shrieks!—the enormous bewilderment at finding herself spasmodically frolicking, they were having their way with her, her pure whiteness suddenly exposed. How many minutes? the minutes of an extended scream of a train rounding the bend, and the joy of another plunge through the air insulting her like a kick, her dancing erratically in the wind, dancing frantically, whether or not she wanted it her body shook like someone laughing, that sensation of laughing to death, the sudden death of someone who had neglected to shred all those papers in the drawer, not the deaths of other people, her own, always her own. She who could have taken advantage of the others screaming to let out her own howl of lament, she forgot herself, all she felt was fright.

And now this silence, sudden too. They'd come back to earth, the machinery once again completely stopped.

Pale, kicked out of a Church, she looked at the stationary earth from which she'd departed and back to which she'd been delivered. She straightened out her skirts primly. She didn't look at anyone. Contrite as on that day when in the middle of everyone the entire contents of her purse had spilled onto the ground and everything that was valuable while lying secretly in her purse, once exposed in the dust of the street, revealed the pettiness of a private life of precautions: face powder, receipt, fountain pen, her retrieving from the curb the scaffolding of her life. She rose from her seat stunned as if shaking off a collision. Though no one was paying attention, she smoothed her skirt again, did what she could so no one would notice how weak and disgraced she was, haughtily protecting her broken bones. But the sky was spinning in her empty stomach; the earth, rising and falling before her eyes, remained distant for a few moments, the earth that is always so troublesome. For a moment the woman wanted, in mutely sobbing fatigue, to reach out her hand to the troublesome earth: her hand reached out like that of a crippled beggar. But as if she had swallowed the void, her heart stunned.

Was that it? That was it. Of the violence, that was it.

She headed back toward the animals. The ordeal of the roller coaster had left her subdued. She didn't make it much further: she had to rest her forehead against the bars of a cage, exhausted, her breath coming quick and shallow. From inside the cage the coati looked at her. She looked at him. Not a single word exchanged. She could never hate that coati who looked at her with the silence of an inquiring body. Disturbed, she averted her eyes from the coati's simplicity. The curious coati asking her a question the way a child asks. And she averting her eyes, concealing from him her deadly mission. Her forehead was pressed against the bars so firmly that for an instant it looked like she was the caged one and a free coati was examining her.

The cage was always on the side she was: she let out a moan that seemed to come from the soles of her feet. After that another moan.

Then, born from her womb, it rose again, beseeching, in a swelling wave, that urge to kill—her eyes welled up grateful and black in a near-happiness, it wasn't hatred yet, for the time being just the tormented urge to hate like a desire, the promise of cruel blossoming, a torment like love, the urge to hate promising itself sacred blood and triumph, the spurned female had become spiritualized through her great hope. But where, where to find the animal that would teach her to have her own hatred? the hatred that was hers by right but that lay excruciatingly out of reach? where could she learn to hate so as not to die of love? And from whom? The world of spring, the world of beasts that in spring Christianize themselves with paws that claw but do not wound … oh no more of this world! no more of this perfume, of this weary panting, no more of this forgiveness in everything that will die one day as if made to surrender. Never forgiveness, if that woman forgave one more time, even just once, her life would be lost—she let out a hoarse, brief moan, the coati gave a start—caged in she looked around, and since she wasn't the kind of person people paid attention to, she crouched down like an old solitary assassin, a child ran past without noticing her.

Then she started walking again, smaller now, tough, fists once again braced in her pockets, the undercover assassin, and everything was caught in her chest. In her chest that knew only how to give up, knew only how to withstand, knew only how to beg forgiveness, knew only how to forgive, that had only learned how to have the sweetness of unhappiness, and learned only how to love, love, love. Imagining that she might never experience the hatred of which her forgiveness had always been made, this caused her heart to moan indecently, she began walking so fast that she seemed to have found a sudden destiny. She was almost running, her shoes throwing her off balance, and giving her a physical fragility that once again reduced her to the imprisoned female, her steps mechanically assumed the beseeching despair of the frail, she who was nothing more than a frail woman herself. But, if she could take off her shoes, could she avoid the joy of walking barefoot? how could you not love the ground on which you walk? She moaned again, stopped before the bars of an enclosure, pressed her hot face against the iron's rusty coolness. Eyes deeply shut she tried to bury her face between the hardness of the railings, her face attempted an impossible passage through the narrow bars, just as before when she'd seen the newborn monkey seek in the blindness of hunger the female's breast. A fleeting comfort came from how the bars seemed to hate her while opposing her with the resistance of frozen iron.

She opened her eyes slowly. Her eyes coming from their own darkness couldn't see a thing in the afternoon's faint light. She stood there breathing. Gradually she started to make things out again, gradually shapes began solidifying, she was tired, crushed by the sweetness of tiredness. Her head tilted inquiringly toward the budding trees, her eyes saw the small white clouds. Without hope, she heard the lightness of a stream. She lowered her head again and stood gazing at the buffalo in the distance. Inside a brown coat, breathing without interest, no one interested in her, she interested in no one.

A certain peace at last. The breeze ruffling the hair on her forehead as if brushing the hair of someone who had just died, whose forehead was still damp with sweat. Gazing detachedly at that great dry plot surrounded by tall railings, the buffalo plot. The black buffalo was standing still at the far end of that plot. Then he paced in the distance on his narrow haunches, his dense haunches. His neck thicker than his tensed flanks. Seen straight on, his large head was broader than his body, blocking the rest from view, like a severed head. And on his head those horns. At a distance he slowly paced with his torso. He was a black buffalo. So black that from afar his face looked feature-less. Atop his blackness the erect stark whiteness of his horns.

The woman might have left but the silence felt good in the waning afternoon.

And in the silence of the paddock, those meandering steps, the dry dust beneath those dry hooves. At a distance, in the midst of his calm pacing, the black buffalo looked at her for an instant. The next instant, the woman again saw only the hard muscle of his body. Maybe he hadn't looked at her. She couldn't tell, since all she could discern of that shadowy head were its outlines. But once more he seemed to have either seen or sensed her.

The woman raised her head a little, retracted it slightly in misgiving. Body motionless, head back, she waited.

And once more the buffalo seemed to notice her.

As if she couldn't stand feeling what she had felt, she suddenly averted her face and looked at a tree. Her heart didn't beat in her chest, her heart was beating hollowly somewhere between her stomach and intestines.

The buffalo made another slow loop. The dust. The woman clenched her teeth, her whole face ached a little.

The buffalo with his constricted torso. In the luminous

dusk he was a body blackened with tranquil rage, the woman sighed slowly. A white thing had spread out inside her, white as paper, fragile as paper, intense as a whiteness. Death droned in her ears. The buffalo's renewed pacing brought her back to herself and, with another long sigh, she returned to the surface. She didn't know where she'd been. She was standing, very feeble, just emerged from that white and remote thing where she'd been.

And from where she looked back at the buffalo.

The buffalo larger now. The black buffalo. Ah, she said suddenly with a pang. The buffalo with his back turned to her, standing still. The woman's whitened face didn't know how to call him. Ah! she said provoking him. Ah! she said. Her face was covered in deathly whiteness, her suddenly gaunt face held purity and veneration. Ah! she goaded him through clenched teeth. But with his back turned, the buffalo completely still.

She grabbed a rock off the ground and hurled it into the paddock. The torso's stillness, quieted down even blacker: the rock rolled away uselessly.

Ah! she said shaking the bars. That white thing was spreading inside her, viscous like a kind of saliva. The buffalo with his back turned.

Ah, she said. But this time because inside her at last was flowing a first trickle of black blood.

The first instant was one of pain. As if the world had convulsed for this blood to flow. She stood there, listening to that first bitter oil drip as in a grotto, the spurned female. Her strength was still trapped between the bars, but something incomprehensible and burning, ultimately incomprehensible, was happening, a thing like a joy tasted in her mouth. Then the buffalo turned toward her.

The buffalo turned, stood still, and faced her from afar.

I love you, she then said with hatred to the man whose great unpunishable crime was not wanting her. I hate you, she said beseeching the buffalo's love.

Provoked at last, the enormous buffalo approached unhurriedly.

He approached, the dust rose. The woman waited with her arms hanging alongside her coat. Slowly he approached. She didn't take a single step back. Until he reached the railings and stopped there. There stood the buffalo and the woman, directly across from each other. She didn't look at his face, or his mouth, or his horns. She looked him in the eye.

And the buffalo's eyes, his eyes looked her in the eye. And such a deep pallor was exchanged that the woman fell into a drowsy torpor. Standing, in a deep sleep. Small red eyes were looking at her. The eyes of the buffalo. The woman was dazed in surprise, slowly shaking her head. The calm buffalo. Slowly the woman was shaking her head, astonished by the hatred with which the buffalo, tranquil with hatred, was looking at her. Nearly absolved, shaking an incredulous head, her mouth slightly open. Innocent, curious, plunging deeper and deeper into those eyes staring unhurriedly at her, simple, with a drowsy sigh, neither wanting nor able to flee, trapped in this mutual murder. Trapped as if her hand were forever stuck to the dagger she herself had thrust. Trapped, as she slid spellbound down the railing. In such slow dizziness that just before her body gently crumpled the woman saw the whole sky and a buffalo.

Monkeys
("Macacos")

THAT FIRST TIME WE HAD A MARMOSET IN THE HOUSE
was around New Year's. We had no running water and no maid,
people were lining up to buy meat, the summer heat had exploded—and that was when, silent with bewilderment, I saw
the present come into the house, already eating a banana, already examining everything with great speed and a long tail. He
seemed more like a big monkey not yet fully grown, he had tre-
mendous potential. He'd climb the laundry hanging on the line,
from where he'd holler like a sailor, and toss banana peels wher-
ever they fell. And I was exhausted. Whenever I'd forget and
wander absentmindedly into the laundry room, the big shock:
that cheerful man was there. My youngest son knew, before I
did, that I would get rid of that gorilla: "And what if I promise
that one day the monkey's going to get sick and die, will you let
him stay? and what if you knew that sooner or later he'll fall out
the window anyway and die down there?" My feelings made me
avert my gaze. The little-big monkey's happy and filthy lack of
awareness made me responsible for his destiny, since he himself wouldn't take the blame. A girlfriend understood of what
bitterness my acquiescence was made, what crimes fed into my

dreamy manner, and crudely saved me: some boys from the favela showed up in a happy commotion, took away the laughing man, and for the lackluster New Year I at least got a monkey-free house.

A year later, I'd just been feeling a surge of joy, when right there in Copacabana I spotted the crowd. A man was selling little monkeys. I thought of the boys, of the joys they gave me for free, unrelated to the worries they also gave me for free, I imagined a circle of joy: "Whoever gets this must pass it on," and on and on, like a chain reaction running up a trail of gunpowder. And right on the spot I bought the one whose name would be Lisette.

She nearly fit in my hand. She was wearing the skirt, earrings, necklace and bracelet of a Bahian woman. And she had the air of an immigrant who lands still dressed in her country's traditional clothing. There was also an immigrant quality in her wide eyes.

As for this one, she was a miniature woman. She spent three days with us. She was so delicately built. And so incredibly sweet. More than just her eyes, her gaze was wide. At every movement, her earrings would tremble; her skirt was always neat, her red necklace shiny. She slept a lot, but was sober and tired when it came to eating. Her rare caresses were just light bites that left no mark.

On the third day we were in the laundry room admiring Lisette and the way she was ours. "A little too gentle," I thought, missing my gorilla. And suddenly my heart replied very sternly: "But that's not sweetness. It's death." The harshness of the message left me speechless. Then I told the boys: "Lisette is dying." Looking at her, I then realized how far our love had gone. I rolled up Lisette in a napkin, went with the boys to the nearest emergency room, where the doctor couldn't see us because he was performing an urgent procedure on a dog. Another taxi—Lisette thinks we're on an outing, Mama—another hospital. There they gave her oxygen.

And with that breath of life, a Lisette we didn't know was suddenly revealed. Her eyes were much less wide, more secretive, more laughing, and her protruding and ordinary face had a certain ironic superiority; a little more oxygen, and she felt like saying that she could hardly stand being a monkey; she was indeed, and had a lot to say. Soon, however, she succumbed once more, exhausted. More oxygen and this time a serum injection to whose prick she reacted with an angry little swipe, her bracelet tinkling. The nurse smiled: "Lisette, dear, calm down!"

The diagnosis: she wasn't going to make it, unless she had oxygen nearby and, even then, it was unlikely. "Don't buy monkeys on the street," he scolded me shaking his head, "sometimes they're already sick." No, you had to buy a good monkey, to know where it came from, for at least five years of guaranteed love, you had to know what it had or hadn't done, as if you were getting married. I talked it over with the boys for a moment. Then I said to the nurse: "Sir, you've taken quite a liking to Lisette. So if you let her spend a couple days near the oxygen, and she gets better, she's yours." But he thought about it. "Lisette is pretty!" I implored. "She's beautiful," he agreed, thoughtful. Then he sighed and said: "If I cure Lisette, she's yours." We left, with an empty napkin.

The next day they called, and I told the boys that Lisette had died. My youngest asked me: "Do you think she died wearing her earrings?" I said yes. A week later my eldest said to me: "You look so much like Lisette!" "I like you too," I replied.

The Egg and the Chicken
("O ovo e a galinha")

IN THE MORNING IN THE KITCHEN ON THE TABLE I SEE the egg.

I look at the egg with a single gaze. Immediately I perceive that one cannot be seeing an egg. Seeing an egg never remains in the present: as soon as I see an egg it already becomes having seen an egg three millennia ago. —At the very instant of seeing the egg it is the memory of an egg. —The egg can only be seen by one who has already seen it. —When one sees the egg it is too late: an egg seen is an egg lost. —Seeing the egg is the promise of one day eventually seeing the egg. —A brief and indivisible glance; if indeed there is thought; there is none; there is the egg. —Looking is the necessary instrument that, once used, I shall discard. I shall keep the egg. —The egg has no itself. Individually it does not exist.

Seeing the egg is impossible: the egg is supervisible just as there are supersonic sounds. No one can see the egg. Does the dog see the egg? Only machines see the egg. The construction crane sees the egg. —When I was ancient an egg landed on my shoulder. —Love for the egg cannot be felt either. Love for the

egg is supersensible. We do not know that we love the egg. —
When I was ancient I was keeper of the egg and I would tread
lightly to avoid upending the egg's silence. When I died, they
removed the egg from me with care. It was still alive. —Only
one who saw the world would see the egg. Like the world, the
egg is obvious.

The egg no longer exists. Like the light of an already-dead
star, the egg properly speaking no longer exists. —You are perfect, egg. You are white. —To you I dedicate the beginning. To
you I dedicate the first time.

To the egg I dedicate the Chinese nation.

The egg is a suspended thing. It has never landed. When
it lands, it is not what has landed. It was a thing under the
egg. —I look at the egg in the kitchen with superficial attention so as not to break it. I take the utmost care not to understand it. Since it is impossible to understand, I know that if
I understand it this is because I am making an error. Understanding is the proof of error. Understanding it is not the way
to see it. —Never thinking about the egg is a way of having
seen it. —I wonder, do I know of the egg? I almost certainly
do. Thus: I exist, therefore I know. —What I don't know
about the egg is what really matters. What I don't know about
the egg gives me the egg properly speaking. —The Moon is
inhabited by eggs.

The egg is an exteriorization. To have a shell is to surrender. —The egg denudes the kitchen. It turns the table into a
slanted plane. The egg exposes. —Whoever plunges deeper
into an egg, whoever sees more than the surface of the egg, is
after something else: that person is hungry.

An egg is the soul of the chicken. The awkward chicken.
The sure egg. The frightened chicken. The sure egg. Like a

paused projectile. For an egg is an egg in space. An egg upon blue. —I love you, egg. I love you as a thing doesn't even know it loves another thing. —I do not touch it. The aura of my fingers is what sees the egg. I do not touch it. —But to dedicate myself to the vision of the egg would be to die to the world, and I need the yolk and the white. —The egg sees me. Does the egg idealize me? Does the egg meditate me? No, the egg merely sees me. It is exempt from the understanding that wounds. —The egg has never struggled. It is a gift. —The egg is invisible to the naked eye. From one egg to another one arrives at God, who is invisible to the naked eye. —The egg could have been a triangle that rolled for so long in space that it became oval. —Is the egg basically a vessel? Could it have been the first vessel sculpted by the Etruscans? No. The egg originated in Macedonia. There it was calculated, fruit of the most arduous spontaneity. In the sands of Macedonia a man holding a stick drew it. And then erased it with his bare foot.

An egg is a thing that must be careful. That's why the chicken is the egg's disguise. The chicken exists so that the egg can traverse the ages. That's what a mother is for. —The egg is constantly persecuted for being too ahead of its time. —An egg, for now, will always be revolutionary. —It lives inside the chicken to avoid being called white. The egg really is white. But it cannot be called white. Not because that harms it, but people who call the egg white, those people die to life. Calling something white that is white can destroy humanity. Once a man was accused of being what he was, and he was called That Man. They weren't lying: He was. But to this day we still haven't recovered, one after the next. The general law for us to stay alive: one can say "a pretty face," but whoever says "the face," dies; for having exhausted the topic.

Over time, the egg became a chicken egg. It is not. But, once it was adopted, it took that name. —One should say "the chicken's egg." If one merely says "the egg," the topic is exhausted, and the world becomes naked. — When it comes to the egg, the danger lies in discovering what might be called beauty, that is, its veracity. The veracity of the egg is not verisimilar. If they find out, they might want to force it to become rectangular. The danger is not for the egg, it wouldn't become rectangular. (Our guarantee is that it is unable: being unable is the egg's great strength: its grandiosity comes from the greatness of being unable, which radiates from it like a not-wanting.) But whoever struggles to make it rectangular would be losing his own life. The egg puts us, therefore, in danger. Our advantage is that the egg is invisible. And as for the initiates, the initiates disguise the egg.

As for the chicken's body, the chicken's body is the greatest proof that the egg does not exist. All you have to do is look at the chicken to make it obvious that the egg cannot possibly exist.

And what about the chicken? The egg is the chicken's great sacrifice. The egg is the cross the chicken bears in life. The egg is the chicken's unattainable dream. The chicken loves the egg. She doesn't know the egg exists. If she knew she had an egg inside her, would she save herself? If she knew she had the egg inside her, she would lose her state of being a chicken. Being a chicken is the chicken's survival. Surviving is salvation. For living doesn't seem to exist. Living leads to death. So what the chicken does is be permanently surviving. Surviving is what's called keeping up the struggle against life that is deadly. That's what being a chicken is. The chicken looks embarrassed.

The chicken must not know she has an egg. Or else she would save herself as a chicken, which is no guarantee either, but she would lose the egg. So she doesn't know. The chicken exists so that the egg can use the chicken. She was only meant to be fulfilled, but she liked it. The chicken's undoing comes from this: liking wasn't part of being born. To like being alive hurts. —As for which came first, it was the egg that found the chicken. The chicken was not even summoned. The chicken is directly singled out. —The chicken lives as if in a dream. She has no sense of reality. All the chicken's fright comes because they're always interrupting her reverie. The chicken is a sound sleep. —The chicken suffers from an unknown ailment. The chicken's unknown ailment is the egg. —She doesn't know how to explain herself: "I know that the error is inside me," she calls her life an error, "I don't know what I feel anymore," etc.

"Etc., etc., etc.," is what the chicken clucks all day long. The chicken has plenty of inner life. To be honest, the only thing the chicken really has is inner life. Our vision of her inner life is what we call "chicken." The chicken's inner life consists of acting as if she understands. At the slightest threat she screams bloody murder like a maniac. All this so the egg won't break inside her. An egg that breaks inside the chicken is like blood.

The chicken looks at the horizon. As if it were from the line of the horizon that an egg is coming. Beyond being a mode of transport for the egg, the chicken is silly, idle and myopic. How could the chicken understand herself if she is the contradiction of an egg? The egg is still the same one that originated in Macedonia. The chicken is always the most modern of tragedies. She is always pointlessly current. And she keeps being redrawn. The most suitable form for a chicken has yet to be found. While my neighbor talks on the phone he redraws the chicken with an absentminded pencil. But there's nothing to be done for the chicken: part of her nature is not to be of use to herself. Given, however, that her destiny is more important than she is, and given that her destiny is the egg, her personal life does not concern us.

Inside herself the chicken doesn't recognize the egg, but neither does she recognize it outside herself. When the chicken sees the egg she thinks she's dealing with something impossible. And with her heart beating, with her heart beating so, she doesn't recognize it.

Suddenly I look at the egg in the kitchen and all I see in it is food. I don't recognize it, and my heart beats. The metamorphosis is happening inside me: I start not to be able to discern the egg anymore. Beyond every particular egg, beyond every egg that's eaten, the egg does not exist. I can now no longer believe in an egg. More and more I lack the strength to believe, I am dying, farewell, I looked at an egg too long and it started putting me to sleep.

The chicken who didn't want to sacrifice her life. The one who chose wanting to be "happy." The one who didn't notice that, if she spent her life drawing the egg inside herself as in an illuminated manuscript, she would be good for something. The one who didn't know how to lose herself. The one who thought she had chicken feathers to cover her because she had precious skin, not understanding that the feathers were meant exclusively for helping her along as she carried the egg, because intense suffering might harm the egg. The one who thought pleasure was a gift to her, not realizing that it was meant to keep her completely distracted while the egg was being formed. The one who didn't know "I" is just one of those words you draw while talking on the phone, a mere attempt to find a better shape. The one who thought "I" means having a one-self. The chickens who harm the egg are those that are a ceaseless "I." In them, the "I" is so constant that they can no longer utter the word "egg." But, who knows, maybe that's exactly what the egg was in need of. For if they weren't so distracted, if they paid attention to the great life forming inside them, they would get in the way of the egg.

I started talking about the chicken and for a while now I have no longer been talking about the chicken. But I'm still talking about the egg.

And thus I don't understand the egg. I only understand a broken egg: I crack it on the frying pan. In this indirect way I give myself to the egg's existence: my sacrifice is reducing myself to my personal life. I turned my pleasure and my pain into my hidden destiny. And having only one's own life is, for those who have already seen the egg, a sacrifice. Like the ones who, in a convent, sweep the floor and do the laundry, serving without the glory of a higher purpose, my job is to live out my pleasures and my pains. I must have the modesty to live.

I pick up another egg in the kitchen, I break its shell and shape. And from this precise moment there was never an egg. It is absolutely essential that I be a busy and distracted person. I am necessarily one of those people who refuse. I belong to that Masonic society of those who once saw the egg and refused it as a way to protect it. We are the ones who abstain from destroying, and by doing so are consumed. We, undercover agents dispersed among less revealing duties, we sometimes recognize each other. By a certain way of looking, by a way of shaking hands, we recognize each other and call this love. And then our disguise is unnecessary: though we don't speak, neither do we lie, though we don't speak the truth, neither must we dissemble any longer. Love is when we are allowed to participate a bit more. Few want love, because love is the great disillusionment with all the rest. And few can bear losing the rest of their illusions. There are people who would volunteer for love, thinking love will enrich their personal lives. On the contrary: love is ultimately poverty. Love is not having. Moreover love is the disillusionment of what you thought was love. And it's no prize, that's why it doesn't make people vain, love is no prize, it's a status granted exclusively to people who, without it, would defile the egg with their personal suffering. That doesn't make love an honorable exception; it is granted precisely to those bad agents, those who would ruin everything if they weren't allowed to guess at things vaguely.

All the agents are granted several advantages so that the egg may form. It is no cause for envy since, even certain statuses, worse than other people's, are merely the ideal conditions for the egg. As for the agents' pleasure, they also receive it without pride. They austerely experience all pleasures: it is even our sacrifice so that the egg may form. Upon us has been imposed, as well, a nature entirely prone to much pleasure. Which makes it easier. At the very least it makes pleasure less arduous.

There are cases of agents committing suicide: they find the minimal instructions they have received insufficient, and feel unsupported. There was the case of the agent who publicly revealed himself as an agent because he found not being understood intolerable, and could no longer stand not being respected by others: he was fatally run over as he was leaving a restaurant. There was another who didn't even have to be eliminated: he was slowly consumed by his own rebellion, his rebellion came when he discovered that the two or three instructions he had received included no explanation whatsoever. There was another, eliminated too, because he thought "the truth should be bravely spoken," and started first of all to seek it out; they say he died in the name of the truth, but in fact he was just making the truth harder with his innocence; his seeming bravery was foolhardiness, and his desire for loyalty was naive, he hadn't understood that being loyal isn't so tidy, being loyal means being disloyal to everything else. Those extreme cases of death aren't caused by cruelty. It's because there's a job, let's call it cosmic, to be done, and individual cases unfortunately cannot be taken into consideration. For those who succumb and become individuals there are institutions, charity, comprehension that doesn't distinguish motives, in a word our human life.

The eggs crackle in the frying pan, and lost in a dream I make breakfast. Lacking any sense of reality, I shout for the children who sprout from various beds, drag the chairs out and eat, and the work of the breaking day begins, shouted and laughed and eaten, white and yolk, merriment amid fighting, the day that is our salt and we are the day's salt, living is extremely tolerable, living keeps us busy and distracts us, living makes us laugh.

And it makes me smile in my mystery. My mystery is that being merely a means, and not an end, has given me the most mischievous of freedoms: I'm no fool and I make the most of things. Even to the point of wronging others so much that, frankly. The fake job they have given me to disguise my true purpose, since I make the most of this fake job and turn it into my real one; this includes the money they give me as a daily allowance to ease my life so that the egg may form, since I have used this money for other purposes, diverting the funds, I recently bought stock in Brahma beer and am rich. All this I still call having the necessary modesty to live. And also the time they have granted me, and that they grant us just so that in this honorable leisure the egg may form, well I have used this time for illicit pleasures and illicit pains, completely forgetting the egg. That is my simplicity.

Or is that exactly what they want to happen to me, precisely so the egg can carry out its mission? Is it freedom or am I being controlled? Because I keep noticing how every error of mine has been put to use. My rebellion is that for them I am nothing, I am merely valuable: they take care of me from one second to the next, with the most absolute lack of love; I am merely valuable. With the money they give me, I have taken to drinking lately. Abuse of trust? But it's because nobody knows how it feels inside for someone whose job consists of pretending that she is betraying, and who ends up believing in her own betrayal. Whose job consists of forgetting every day. Someone of whom apparent dishonor is required. Not even my mirror still reflects a face that is mine. Either I am an agent, or it really is betrayal.

Yet I sleep the sleep of the righteous because I know that my futile life doesn't interfere with the march of great time. On the contrary: it seems that I am required to be extremely futile, I'm even required to sleep like one of the righteous. They want me busy and distracted, and they don't care how. Because, with my misguided attention and grave foolishness, I could interfere with whatever is carried out through me. It's because I myself, I properly speaking, all I have really been good for is interfering. What tells me that I might be an agent is the idea that my destiny surpasses me: at least they really did have to let me guess that, I was one of those people who would do their job badly if they couldn't guess at least a little; they made me forget what they had let me guess, but I still had the vague notion that my destiny surpasses me, and that I am an instrument of their work. But in any case all I could be was an instrument, since the work couldn't really be mine. I have already tried to strike out on my own and it didn't work out; my hand trembles to this day. Had I kept at it any longer I would have damaged my health forever. Since then, ever since that thwarted experiment, I have tried to consider things this way: that much has already been given me, that they have granted me everything that might be granted; and that other agents, far superior to me, have also worked solely for something they did not know. And with the same minimal instructions. Much has already been given me; this, for example: every once in a while, with my heart beating at the privilege, I at least know that I am not recognizing anything! with my heart beating from emotion, I at least do not understand! with my heart beating from trust, I at least do not know.

But what about the egg? This is one of their ploys: while I was talking about the egg, I had forgotten the egg. "Talk, talk!" they instructed me. And the egg is fully protected by all those words. Keep talking, is one of the instructions, I am so tired.

Out of devotion to the egg, I forgot it. My necessary forgetting. My self-serving forgetting. Because the egg is an evasion. In the face of my possessive adoration it could retreat and never again return. But if it is forgotten. If I make the sacrifice of living only my life and of forgetting it. If the egg becomes impossible. Then—free, delicate, with no message for me—perhaps one last time it will move from space over to this window that I have always left open. And at dawn it will descend into our building. Serene all the way to the kitchen. Illuminating it with my pallor.

Temptation

("Tentação")

SHE WAS SOBBING. AND AS IF THE TWO O'CLOCK GLARE
weren't enough, she had red hair.

On the empty street the cobblestones were vibrating with
heat—the little girl's head was aflame. Sitting on the front
steps of her house, she endured. Nobody on the street, just
one person waiting in vain at the tram stop. And as if her submissive and patient gaze weren't enough, her sobs kept interrupting her, making her chin slip off the hand it was resting
on in resignation. What could you do about a sobbing red-
haired girl? We looked at each other wordlessly, dejection to
dejection. On the deserted street not a sign of the tram. In a
land of dark-haired people, being a redhead was an involun-
tary rebellion. What did it matter if one day in the future her
emblem would make her insolently hold erect the head of a
woman. For now she was sitting on a shimmering doorstep,
at two o'clock. What saved her was an old purse, with a torn
strap. She clutched it with a long-familiar conjugal love, press-
ing it against her knees.

That was when her other half in this world approached, a

brother in Grajaú. The possibility of communication appeared at the scorching angle of the street corner, accompanied by a lady, and incarnated in the form of a dog. It was a basset hound, beautiful and miserable, sweet inside its fate. It was a red-haired basset hound.

There he came trotting, ahead of his owner, elongating his body. Unsuspecting, nonchalant, dog.

The girl widened her eyes in amazement. Mildly alerted, the dog stopped in front of her. His tongue quivered. They looked at each other.

Of all the beings suited to become the owner of another being, there sat the girl who had come into this world to have that dog. He growled gently, without barking. She looked at him from under her hair, fascinated, solemn. How much time passed? A big sob jangled her. He didn't even tremble. She overcame her sobs and kept staring at him.

Both had short, red hair.

What did they say to each other? Nobody knows. All we know is they communicated rapidly, since there was no time. We also know that without speaking they were asking for each other. They were asking for each other urgently, bashfully, surprised.

Amid so much vague impossibility and so much sun, here was the solution for the red child. And amid so many streets to be trotted down, so many bigger dogs, so many dry gutters—there sat a little girl, as if she were flesh of his ginger flesh. They stared at each other deeply, immersed, absent from Grajaú. Another second and the suspended dream would shatter, yielding perhaps to the seriousness with which they asked for one another.

But both were already committed.

She to her impossible childhood, the center of the innocence that would only open once she was a woman. He, to his imprisoned nature.

His owner waited impatiently beneath her parasol. The red-haired basset finally pried himself away from the girl and went off sleepwalking. She sat there in shock, holding the event in her hands, in a muteness that neither her father nor mother would understand. She followed him with black eyes that could hardly believe it, hunched over her purse and knees, until she saw him round the next corner.

But he was stronger than she. He didn't look back once.

Journey to Petrópolis
("Viagem a Petrópolis")

SHE WAS A WITHERED LITTLE OLD LADY WHO, SWEET
and stubborn, didn't seem to understand that she was alone in
the world. Her eyes were always tearing up, her hands rested
on her dull black dress, an old document of her life. On the
now-stiff fabric were little bread crumbs stuck on by the drool
that was now resurfacing, recalling the cradle. There was a
yellowish stain, from an egg she'd eaten two weeks before.
And marks from the places where she slept. She always found
somewhere to sleep, at someone or other's house. Whenever
they asked her name, she'd say in a voice purified by frailty and
countless years of good manners:
"Missy."
People would smile. Pleased at sparking their interest, she'd
explain:
"My name, my real name, is Margarida."
Her body was small, dark, though she'd been tall and fair.
She'd had a father, mother, husband, two children. All had died
one after the other. Only she remained, with her rheumy, expectant eyes nearly covered by a velvety white film. Whenever
anyone gave her money it was very little, since she was small

and really didn't need to eat much. Whenever they gave her a bed to sleep in they gave her a hard, narrow one because Margarida was gradually losing mass. Nor did she offer much thanks: she'd smile and nod.

Nowadays she was sleeping, no one remembered why, in a room behind a big house, on a broad, tree-lined street in Botafogo. The family thought Missy was quaint but forgot her most of the time. It was because she was also a mysterious old lady. She rose at the crack of dawn, made up her dwarf's bed and darted out nimbly as if the house were on fire. Nobody knew where she went. One day one of the girls of the house asked her what she was doing. She answered with a pleasant smile:

"Strolling around."

They thought it quaint that an old lady, living off charity, would stroll around. But it was true. Missy was born in Maranhão, where she had always lived. She'd come to Rio not long before, with a very nice lady who'd been planning to put her in a nursing home, but it didn't work out: the lady went to Minas Gerais and gave Missy some money to set herself up in Rio. And the old woman strolled around getting to know the city. All you had to do anyhow was sit on a park bench and you'd already be seeing Rio de Janeiro.

Her life was going along smoothly, when one day the family from the Botafogo house was surprised that she'd been in their home so long, and thought it was too much. In a way they were right. Everyone there was very busy, every so often weddings, parties, engagements, visits came up. And whenever they rushed busily past the old lady, they'd start as if they'd been interrupted, accosted with a swipe on the shoulder: "hey!" In particular one of the girls of the house felt an irritated distress, the old lady annoyed her for no reason. In particular her permanent

smile, though the girl understood it was just an inoffensive ric-
tus. Perhaps because they didn't have time, no one brought it
up. But as soon as someone thought of sending her to Petrópolis, to their German sister-in-law's house, there came a more
enthusiastic consensus than an old lady could have provoked.

So, when the son of the house took his girlfriend and two
sisters for a weekend in Petrópolis, they brought the old lady
along in the car.

Why didn't Missy sleep the night before? At the idea of a
trip, in her stiff body her heart lost its rust, all dry and skipping
a beat, as if she'd swallowed a large pill without water. There
were moments when she couldn't even breathe. She talked all
night long, sometimes loudly. Her excitement about the promised outing and the change in her life suddenly cleared up some
of her ideas. She remembered things that a few days before she'd
have sworn never existed. Starting with her son who was run
over, killed by a tram in Maranhão—if he had lived amid the
traffic of Rio de Janeiro, then he'd really have been run over. She
remembered her son's hair, his clothing. She remembered the
teacup Maria Rosa had broken and how she'd yelled at Maria
Rosa. If she had known her daughter would die in childbirth, of
course she wouldn't have needed to yell. And she remembered
her husband. She could only recall her husband in shirtsleeves.
But that couldn't be, she was sure he went to the office in his
clerk uniform, he'd go to parties in a sport coat, not to mention
that he couldn't have gone to the funerals of his son and daughter in shirtsleeves. Searching for her husband's sport coat tired
the old lady out further as she tossed and turned lightly in bed.
Suddenly she discovered that the mattress was hard.

"What a hard mattress," she said very loudly in the middle
of the night.

What happened is that all her senses had returned. Parts of her body she hadn't been aware of in a long time were now clamoring for her attention. And all of a sudden—oh what raging hunger! Hallucinating, she got up, unfastened her little bundle, took out a stale piece of buttered bread she had secretly kept for two days. She ate the bread like a rat, scratching up the places in her mouth that had only gums until they bled. And thanks to the food, she felt increasingly reinvigorated. She managed, though fleetingly, to catch a vision of her husband saying goodbye on his way to work. Only after the memory vanished did she notice she'd forgotten to check whether he was in shirtsleeves. She lay down again, scratching her searing body all over. She spent the rest of the night in this pattern of seeing for an instant and then not managing to see anymore. Near dawn she fell asleep.

And for the very first time she had to be roused. While it was still dark, the girl came to get her, kerchief tied around her head and suitcase already in hand. Unexpectedly Missy asked for a few seconds to comb her hair. Her tremulous hands held the broken comb. She combed her hair, combed her hair. She'd never been the kind of woman who went out without first combing her hair thoroughly.

When she finally approached the car, the young man and the girls were surprised by her cheerful manner and sprightly step. "She's healthier than I am!" the young man joked. The thought occurred to the girl of the house: "And to think I was even feeling sorry for her."

Missy sat by the car window, a little crowded by the two sisters squeezed onto the same backseat. She didn't say anything, smiling. But when the car jerked into motion, launching her backward, she felt pain in her chest. It wasn't just from joy, it was tearing at her. The young man turned around:

"Don't get sick, Granny!"

The girls laughed, especially the one who'd sat in front, the one who occasionally leaned her head on the young man's shoulder. Out of politeness, the old lady wanted to answer, but couldn't. She wanted to smile, she couldn't. She looked at everyone, teary-eyed, which the others already knew didn't mean she was crying. Something in her face somewhat deadened the joy the girl of the house felt and lent her a stubborn expression.

It was quite a lovely journey.

The girls were pleased, Missy had started smiling again. And, though her heart was racing, everything was better. They drove past a cemetery, past a grocery store, tree, two women, a soldier, cat! signs—everything swallowed up by speed.

When Missy awoke she no longer knew where she was. The highway was now in broad daylight: it was narrow and dangerous. The old lady's mouth stung, her frozen feet and hands were growing distant from the rest of her body. The girls were talking, the one in front had rested her head on the young man's shoulder. Their belongings were constantly tumbling down.

Then Missy's head started working. Her husband appeared to her in a sport coat—I found it, I found it! the sport coat had been on a hanger the whole time. She remembered the name of Maria Rosa's friend, the one who lived across the street: Elvira, and Elvira's mother was even crippled. The memories nearly wrenched a shout from her. Then she moved her lips slowly and murmured a few words.

The girls were talking:

"Well, thank you very much, I won't accept a present like that!"

That's when Missy finally started not to understand. What was she doing in the car? how had she met her husband and where? how did Maria Rosa and Rafael's mother, their very own mother, end up in a car with these people? A moment later she was used to it again.

The young man said to his sisters:

"I think it's better not to park in front, to avoid gossip. She'll get out of the car, we'll show her where it is, she'll go by herself and tell them she's supposed to stay."

One of the girls of the house felt uneasy: she worried that her brother, being dense like a typical man, would say too much in front of his girlfriend. They didn't visit their brother in Petrópolis anymore, and saw their sister-in-law even less.

"Right," she broke in just before he said too much. "Look, Missy, go down that alley and you can't miss it: at the red-brick house, you ask for Arnaldo, my brother, okay? Arnaldo. Say you couldn't stay with us anymore, say there's room at Arnaldo's and you could even look after their boy sometimes, okay ..."

Missy got out of the car, and for a while kept standing there but floating dizzily above wheels. The cool wind blew her long skirt between her legs.

Arnaldo wasn't home. Missy entered the alcove where the lady of the house, with a dust rag tied around her head, was having breakfast. A blond boy—surely the one Missy was supposed to look after—was seated in front of a plate of tomatoes and onions and eating drowsily, while his white, freckled legs were swinging under the table. The German woman filled his dish with oatmeal, pushed buttered toast across the table to him. The flies were buzzing. Missy felt faint. If she drank some hot coffee maybe the chill in her body would go away.

The German woman examined her silently every so often: she hadn't believed the story about her sister-in-law's suggestion, though "from them" anything was possible. But maybe the old lady had heard the address from someone, maybe even on a tram, by chance, that sometimes happened, all you had to do was open the newspaper and see the things that went on. It was just that the story wasn't very convincing, and the old lady had a sly look, she didn't even hide her smile. Best not to leave her alone in the alcove with the cupboard full of new dishes.

"First I have to eat breakfast," she told her. "After my husband gets home, we'll see what can be done."

Missy didn't understand very well, because the woman spoke like a foreigner. But she understood that she was to stay seated. The smell of coffee gave her a craving, and a dizziness that darkened the whole room. Her lips stung drily and her heart beat completely independently. Coffee, coffee, she looked on, smiling and tearing up. At her feet the dog was gnawing at its own paw, growling. The maid, also somewhat foreign, tall, with a very slender neck and large breasts, the maid brought a plate of soft white cheese. Wordlessly, the mother smashed a hunk of cheese onto the toast and pushed it over to her son's side of the table. The boy ate it all and, with his belly sticking out, grabbed a toothpick and stood:

"Mother, gimme a hundred cruzeiros."

"No. For what?"

"Chocolate."

"No. Sunday's not till tomorrow."

A flicker lit up Missy: Sunday? what was she doing in that house on the eve of the Sabbath? She could never have guessed. But she'd be pleased to look after that boy. She'd always liked blond children: all blond boys looked like the Baby Jesus. What was she doing in that house? They kept making her move from place to place for no reason, but she'd tell about everything, they'd see. She smiled sheepishly: she wouldn't tell on them at all, since what she really wanted was coffee.

The lady of the house shouted toward another room, and the indifferent maid brought out a bowl, filled with dark mush. Foreigners sure ate a lot in the morning, Missy had witnessed as much in Maranhão. The lady of the house, with her no-nonsense manner, because foreigners in Petrópolis were just as serious as they were in Maranhão, the lady of the house took a spoonful of white cheese, mashed it with her fork and mixed it into the mush. Honestly, it really was foreign slop. She then started eating, absorbed, with the same look of distaste foreigners in Maranhão have. Missy watched. The dog growled at its fleas.

Finally Arnaldo appeared in full sunlight, the crystal cabinet sparkling. He wasn't blond. He spoke with his wife in a hushed voice, and after a drawn-out discussion informed Missy firmly and carefully: "It's just not possible, there's just no room here."

And since the old lady didn't object and kept on smiling, he said it louder:

"There's just no room, okay?"

But Missy remained seated. Arnaldo half gestured. He looked at the two women in the room and got a vague sense of the comic nature of the contrast. His wife taut and ruddy. And past her the old lady shriveled and dark, with folds of dry skin drooping from her shoulders. Faced with the old lady's mischievous smile, he lost patience:

"And I'm very busy now! I'll give you some money and you take the train to Rio, okay? go back to my mother's house, and when you get there say: Arnaldo's house isn't an old folks' home, okay? there's no room here. Say this: Arnaldo's house isn't an old folks' home, okay!"

Missy took the money and headed for the door. When Arnaldo was just sitting down to eat, Missy reappeared:

"Thank you, may God help you."

Out on the street, she thought once more of Maria Rosa, Rafael, her husband. She didn't miss them the slightest bit. But she remembered. She headed for the highway, getting farther and farther from the station. She smiled as if playing a trick on somebody: instead of heading back right away, she'd take a little stroll first. A man walked by. Then a very odd and utterly unimportant thing was illuminated: when she was still a woman, men. She couldn't manage to get an exact image of the men's faces, but she saw herself in pale blouses with long hair. Her thirst returned, burning her throat. The sun flamed, sparkling on every white pebble. The Petrópolis highway is quite lovely.

At the wet black stone fountain, right on the highway, a barefoot black woman was filling a can of water.

Missy stood still, watching. Then she saw the black woman cup her hands and drink.

Once the highway was empty again, Missy darted out as if emerging from a hiding place and stole up to the fountain. The rivulets of water ran icily into her sleeves up to her elbows, tiny droplets glistened, caught in her hair.

Her thirst quenched, stunned, she kept strolling, eyes widened, focused on the violent churning of the heavy water inside her stomach, awakening little reflexes throughout the rest of her body like lights.

The highway climbed quite a bit. The highway was lovelier than Rio de Janeiro, and climbed quite a bit. Missy sat on a rock beside a tree, to admire it all. The sky was incredibly high, without a cloud. And there were many little birds flying from the chasm toward the highway. The sun-bleached highway extended along a green chasm. Then, since she was tired, the old lady rested her head on the trunk of the tree and died.

The Fifth Story

("A quinta história")

THIS STORY COULD BE CALLED "THE STATUES." AN-
other possible name is "The Murder." And also "How to Kill
Cockroaches." So I will tell at least three stories, all true because they don't contradict each other. Though a single story,
they would be a thousand and one, were I given a thousand
and one nights.

The first, "How to Kill Cockroaches," begins like this: I
was complaining about cockroaches. A lady overheard me.
She gave me this recipe for killing them. I was to mix equal
parts sugar, flour and plaster. The flour and sugar would attract them, the plaster would dry up their insides. That's what
I did. They died.

The other story is actually the first one and is called "The
Murder." It begins like this: I was complaining about cockroaches. A lady overheard me. The recipe follows. And then
comes the murder. The truth is that I was only complaining
about cockroaches in the abstract, since they weren't even
mine: they belonged to the ground floor and would crawl up
the building's pipes to our home. Only once I prepared the mix-
ture did they become mine too. In our name, then, I began to

measure and weigh the ingredients with a slightly more intense concentration. A vague resentment had overtaken me, a sense of outrage. By day the cockroaches were invisible and no one would believe in the secret curse that gnawed at such a peaceful home. But if they, like secret curses, slept during the day, there I was preparing their evening poison. Meticulous, ardent, I concocted the elixir for drawn-out death. An excited fear and my own secret curse guided me. Now I icily wanted just one thing: to kill every cockroach in existence. Cockroaches crawl up the pipes while we, worn out, dream. And now the recipe was ready, so white. As if for cockroaches as clever as I was, I expertly spread the powder until it looked more like something from nature. From my bed, in the silence of the apartment, I imagined them crawling one by one up to the laundry room where the darkness was sleeping, just one towel alert on the clothesline. I awoke hours later with a start when I realized how late it was. It was already dawn. I crossed the kitchen. There they were on the laundry-room floor, hard, huge. During the night I had killed. In our name, day was breaking. Up in the favela a rooster crowed.

The third story that now begins is the one about the "Statues." It begins by saying that I had been complaining about cockroaches. Then comes the same lady. It keeps going up to the point where, near dawn, I awake and still sleepy cross the kitchen. Even sleepier than I is the room from the perspective of its tile floor. And in the darkness of dawn, a purplish glow that distances everything, I discern at my feet shadows and white forms: dozens of statues scattered, rigid. The cockroaches that have hardened from the inside out. Some, belly up. Others, in the middle of a gesture never to be completed. In the mouths of some a bit of the white food. I am the first witness of daybreak in Pompeii. I know how this last night went, I know of the orgy in the dark. Inside some of them the plaster will have hardened as slowly as during some vital process, and they, with increasingly arduous movements, will have greedily intensified the night's joys, trying to escape their own insides. Until they turn to stone, in innocent shock, and with such, such a look of wounded reproach. Others—suddenly assaulted by their own core, without even the slightest inkling that some internal mold was being petrified!—these suddenly crystallize, the way a word is cut off in the mouth: it's you I … They who, taking the name of love in vain, kept singing through the summer night. Whereas that one there, the one whose brown antenna is smeared with white, must have figured out too late that it had been mummified precisely for not having known how to make use of things with the gratuitous charm of being in vain: "because I looked too deep inside myself! because I looked too deep inside …"—from my cold, human height I look at the destruction of a world. Day breaks. The occasional antenna of a dead cockroach quivers drily in the breeze. From the previous story the rooster crows.

The fourth narrative inaugurates a new era at home. It begins as we know: I was complaining about cockroaches. It goes up to the moment I see the plaster monuments. Dead, yes. But I look toward the pipes, from where this very night a slow and living population will renew itself in single file. So would I renew the lethal sugar every night? like someone who can no longer sleep without the eagerness of a rite. And every dawn lead myself to the pavilion with the compulsion of greeting the statues that my sweaty night has been erecting. I trembled with wicked pleasure at the vision of that double life of a sorceress. And I also trembled at the sign of plaster drying: the compulsion to live that would burst my internal mold. A harsh instant of choosing between two paths that, I thought, are bidding each other farewell, and sure that either choice would be a sacrifice: me or my soul. I chose. And today I secretly boast in my heart a plaque of virtue: "This house has been disinfested."

The fifth story is called "Leibniz and the Transcendence of Love in Polynesia." It begins like this: I was complaining about cockroaches.

The Foreign Legion
("A legião estrangeira")

IF ANYONE ASKED ME ABOUT OFÉLIA AND HER PAR-
ents, I'd have answered with the decorum of honesty: I hardly
knew them. Before the same jury I'd answer: I hardly know
myself—and to every face in the jury I'd say with the same
clear-eyed look of someone hypnotized into obedience: I
hardly know you. Yet sometimes I awake from a long slumber
and I meekly turn to the delicate abyss of disorder.

I am trying to talk about that family that disappeared years
ago without leaving a trace in me, and of whom all I've retained
is an image tinged green by distance. My unexpected consent
to know was provoked today by the fact that a chick turned
up in the house. It was brought by a hand that wanted the
pleasure of giving me something born. As soon as we released
the chick, its charm took us by surprise. Tomorrow is Christmas, but the moment of silence I await all year came a day
before Christ's birth. A thing peeping on its own rouses that
ever so gentle curiosity that beside a manger is worship. Well,
well, said my husband, and now look at that. He'd felt too big.
Dirty, mouths open, the boys approached. I, feeling a bit daring, was happy. The chick, it kept peeping. But Christmas

is tomorrow, my older boy said bashfully. We were smiling helplessly, curious.

Yet feelings are the water of an instant. Soon—as the same water is already different when the sun turns it clear, and different when it gets riled up trying to bite a stone, and different over a submerged foot—soon our faces no longer held only aura and illumination. Surrounding the woeful chick, we were kind and anxious. With my husband, kindness makes him gruff and severe, which we're used to; he crucifies himself a bit. In the boys, who are more solemn, kindness is a kind of ardor. With me, kindness intimidates. In a little while the same water was different, and we watched with strained looks, tangled in our clumsiness at being good. And, the water different still, gradually our faces held the responsibility of a yearning, hearts heavy with a love that was no longer free. What also threw us off was the chick's fear of us; there we were, and none of us deserved to be in the presence of a chick; with every peep, it scattered us back. With every peep, it reduced us to doing nothing. The steadiness of its fright accused us of a frivolous joy that by then was no longer even joy, it was vexation. The chick's moment had passed, and it, ever more urgently, was expelling us without letting us go. We, the adults, had already shut down our feelings. But in the boys there was a silent indignation, and their accusation was that we were doing nothing for the chick or for humanity. With us, father and mother, the increasingly endless peeping had already led to an embarrassed resignation: that's just how things are. But we had never told the boys this, we were ashamed; and we'd been putting off indefinitely the moment to call them and explain clearly that's how things are. It got harder every time, the silence would grow, and they'd slightly push away the eagerness with which we wanted to offer them, in exchange, love.

Since we'd never discussed these things, now we had to hide from them all the more the smiling that ultimately came over us at the desperate peeping from that beak, smiling as if it were up to us to bless the fact that this was just how things are, and we had newly blessed them.

The chick, it kept peeping. On the polished table it didn't venture a step, a movement, it peeped inwardly. I didn't even know where there was room for all that terror in a thing made only of feathers. Feathers covering what? a half dozen bones that had come together weakly for what? for the peeping of a terror. In silence, respecting the impossibility of understanding ourselves, respecting the boys' revolt against us, in silence we watched without much patience. It was impossible to offer it that reassuring word that would make it not be afraid, to console a thing frightened because it was born. How could we promise it would get used to things? A father and mother, we knew how fleeting the chick's life would be. It knew as well, in that way that living things know: through profound fright.

And meanwhile, the chick full of grace, brief and yellow thing. I wanted for it too to feel the grace of its life, just as we'd been asked to, that being who was a joy for others, not for itself. For it to feel that it was gratuitous, not even necessary—one chick has to be useless—it had been born only for the glory of God, thus it was the joy of men. Yet wanting the chick to be happy just because we loved it was loving our own love. I also knew that only a mother can resolve birth, and ours was the love of those who rejoice in loving: I was caught up in the grace of having been allowed to love, bells, bells ringing because I know how to worship. But the chick was trembling, a thing of terror, not beauty.

The youngest boy couldn't bear it any longer:

"Do you want to be its mother?"

I said yes, startled. I was the envoy dispatched to that thing that didn't understand my only language: I was loving without being loved. The mission could fail, and the eyes of four boys awaited with the intransigence of hope my first effective gesture of love. I retreated a little, smiling in total solitude, looked at my family, wanting them to smile. A man and four boys were staring at me, incredulous and trusting. I was the woman of the house, the granary. Why this impassiveness from the five of them, I didn't get it. How often I must have failed to cause, in my moment of shyness, them to be looking at me. I tried to isolate myself from the challenge of the five men so that I too would put hope in myself and remember what love is like. I opened my mouth, about to tell them the truth: I don't know how.

But what if a woman came to me at night. What if she were holding her son in her lap. And said: heal my son. I'd say: how is it done? She'd answer: heal my son. I'd say: I don't know how either. She'd reply: heal my son. So then—so then because I don't know how to do anything and because I don't remember anything and because it is night—so then I reach out my hand and save a child. Because it is night, because I am alone in someone else's night, because this silence is too great for me, because I have two hands in order to sacrifice the better one and because I have no choice.

So I reached out my hand and picked up the chick.

In that moment I saw Ofélia again. And in that moment I remembered that I had borne witness to a little girl.

Later I remembered how the neighbor, Ofélia's mother, was dusky like a Hindu. She had purplish circles under her eyes that greatly heightened her beauty and gave her an air of fatigue that made men give her a second look. One day, on a bench in the square, while the children were playing, she'd told me with that head of hers, obstinate as someone gazing at the desert: "I've always wanted to take a cake-decorating class." I recalled that her husband—dusky too, as if they'd chosen each other for the dryness of their color—wished to move up in life through his business interests: hotel management or even ownership, I never quite understood. Which gave him a stiff politeness. Whenever we were forced into more prolonged contact in the elevator, he'd accept our exchange of words in a tone of arrogance he brought from greater struggles. By the time we reached the tenth floor, the humility his coldness forced on me had already calmed him somewhat; perhaps he arrived home more satisfied. As for Ofélia's mother, she was afraid that our living on the same floor would create some kind of intimacy and, without knowing that I too kept to myself, avoided me. Our only moment of intimacy had occurred on that park bench, where, with the dark circles under her eyes and her thin mouth, she'd talked about decorating cakes. I hadn't known how to respond and ended up saying, so she'd know I liked her, that I'd enjoy that cake class. That single moment in common distanced us even more, for fear of an abuse of understanding. Ofélia's mother even turned rude in the elevator: the next day I was holding one of the boys by the hand, the elevator was slowly descending, and I, oppressed by the silence that, with the other woman there, was strengthening—said in a pleasant voice that I also immediately found repugnant:

"We're on our way to his grandmother's."

And she, to my shock:

"I didn't ask you anything, I never stick my nose in my neighbors' business."

"Well," I said softly.

Which, right there in the elevator, made me think that I was paying for having been her confidante for a minute on the park bench. Which, in turn, made me think she might have figured that she'd confided more than she actually had. Which, in turn, made me wonder whether she hadn't in fact told me more than either of us realized. As the elevator kept descending and stopping, I reconstructed her insistent and dreamy look on the park bench—and looked with new eyes at the haughty beauty of Ofélia's mother. "I won't tell anyone you want to decorate cakes," I thought glancing at her.

The father aggressive, the mother keeping to herself. An imperious family. They treated me as if I already lived in their future hotel and were offended that I hadn't paid. Above all they treated me as if I neither believed, nor could they prove who they were. And who were they? I wondered sometimes. Why that slap imprinted on their faces, why that exiled dynasty? And they so failed to forgive me that I acted unforgiven: if I ran into them on the street, beyond my circumscribed sector, it took me by surprise, caught red-handed: I'd stand aside to let them pass, give them the right of way—all three, dusky and dressed up, would walk by as if on their way to mass, that family that lived under the sign of some pride or concealed martyrdom, purple-hued like passion flowers. An ancient family, that one.

But our contact happened through the daughter. She was an extremely beautiful little girl, with long, stiff curls, Ofélia, with dark circles under her eyes just like her mother's, the same purplish gums, the same thin mouth like a slit. But this one, the mouth, spoke. It led to her showing up at my place.

She'd ring the doorbell, I'd open the peephole, not see anything, hear a resolute voice:

"It's me, Ofélia Maria dos Santos Aguiar."

Disheartened, I'd open the door. Ofélia would come in. The visit was for me, since back then my two boys were too young for her drawn-out wisdom. I was grown up and busy, but the visit was for me: with an entirely inward focus, as if there were time enough for everything, she'd carefully lift her ruffled skirt, sit down, arrange her ruffles—and only then look at me. As for me, then in the process of transcribing the office records, I'd work and listen. As for Ofélia, she'd give me advice. She had a clear opinion about everything. Everything I did was a bit wrong, in her opinion. She'd say "in my opinion" in an offended tone, as if I should have asked her advice and, since I didn't, she gave it. With her eight haughty and experienced years, she'd say that in her opinion I wasn't raising the boys properly; because give boys an inch and they'll take miles. Never mix bananas and milk. It's deadly. But of course you do whatever you like, ma'am; to each his own. It was too late to be in your bathrobe; her mother changed clothes as soon as she got out of bed, but everyone ends up leading the life they want to live. If I explained that it was because I hadn't yet showered, Ofélia wouldn't say anything, watching me intently. Somewhat gently, then, somewhat patiently, she'd add that it was too late not to have showered. I never got the last word. What last word could I offer when she'd tell me: vegetable pies don't have a top crust. One afternoon at a bakery I found myself unexpectedly confronted with the pointless truth: there with no top crust was a row of vegetable pies. "I told you so," I heard as if she were right there. With her curls and ruffles, with her firm delicacy, she brought an inquisition into the still-messy living room. What mattered was that she also talked a lot of non-sense, which, in my despondency, made me smile hopelessly.

The worst part of the inquisition was the silence. I'd lift my eyes from the typewriter and have no idea how long Ofélia had been silently watching me. What about me could possibly attract that little girl? I wondered in exasperation. Once, after her long silence, she calmly told me: ma'am, you're weird. And I, struck squarely in my unsheltered face—of all things in the face that, being our insides, is such a sensitive thing—I, struck squarely, thought angrily: I'll bet it's that weirdness that brings you around. She who was completely sheltered, and had a sheltered mother, and a sheltered father.

I still preferred, anyhow, advice and criticism. What was less tolerable was her habit of using the word *therefore* to connect clauses in an unerring concatenation. She told me that I had bought too many vegetables at the market—therefore—they wouldn't fit in that small refrigerator and—therefore—they'd wilt before the next market day. Days later I stood looking at the wilted vegetables. Therefore, yes. Another time she had noticed fewer vegetables scattered on the kitchen table, I who had covertly obeyed. Ofélia stared, stared. She seemed on the verge of not saying anything. I stood waiting, combative, mute. Ofélia remarked in an even tone:

"That's not enough to last until the next market day."

The vegetables ran out halfway through the week. How does she know? I wondered curiously. "Therefore" could have been the answer. Why did I never, ever know? Why did she know everything, why was the earth so familiar to her, and I unsheltered? Therefore? Therefore.

One time Ofélia made a mistake. Geography—she said sitting across from me with her fingers clasped in her lap—is a way of studying. It wasn't exactly a mistake, it was more of a slightly cross-eyed thought—but for me it held the charm of a fall, and before the moment faded, I inwardly told her: that's exactly how it's done, just like that! keep going slowly like that, and one day it'll be easier or harder for you, but that's how it is, keep making mistakes, very, very slowly.

One morning, in mid-discussion, she informed me author-itatively: "I'm going home to check on something but I'll be right back." I ventured: "If you're really busy, you don't have to come back." Ofélia stared at me mute, inquisitive. "There goes a very unlikeable little girl," I thought very clearly so she could see the entire statement exposed on my face. She kept staring. A stare in which—with surprise and sorrow—I saw faithful-ness, patient trust in me and the silence of someone who never spoke. When had I thrown her a bone to make her mutely fol-low me for the rest of her life? I looked away. She sighed calmly. And said even more resolutely: "I'll be right back." What does she want?—I got worked up—why do I attract people who don't even like me?

Once, when Ofélia was sitting there, someone rang the doorbell. I went to answer it and found Ofélia's mother. There she stood, protective, demanding:

"Is Ofélia Maria there by any chance?"

"She is," I excused myself as if I had kidnapped her.

"Don't do this anymore," she said to Ofélia in a voice di-rected at me; then she turned to me and, suddenly offended: "Sorry for the inconvenience."

"Not at all, this little girl is so clever."

Her mother looked at me in mild surprise—but suspicion flickered in her eyes. And in them I read: what do you want from her?

"I've already told Ofélia Maria she's not allowed to bother you," she said now with open distrust. And firmly grabbing the girl's hand to take her away, she seemed to be defending her against me. With a feeling of decadence, I peered through the peephole I cracked open without a sound: there they went down the hallway to their apartment, the mother covering her daughter with lovingly murmured scolding, the daughter impassive with her curls and ruffles bobbing. Closing the peephole I realized I hadn't yet changed clothes and, therefore, had been witnessed in that state by the mother who changed clothes as soon as she got out of bed. I thought somewhat unapologetically: well, now the mother looks down on me, therefore I'm rid of that girl ever coming back.

But she kept coming back. I was too attractive to that child. I had plenty of flaws for her advice, I was fertile ground for her to cultivate her severity, I'd already become the domain of that slave of mine: she kept coming back, lifting her ruffles, sitting down.

On that occasion, because it was almost Easter, the market was full of chicks, and I brought one home for the boys. We played with it, then it stayed in the kitchen, the boys went outside. Later Ofélia showed up for a visit. I was typing away, distractedly giving in every so often. The girl's steady voice, the voice of someone reciting by heart, was making me a little dizzy, slipping in among the written words; she kept talking, kept talking.

That's when it struck me that everything had suddenly stopped. Sensing a lack of torture, I looked at her hazily. Ofélia Maria was holding her head erect, her curls completely still.

"What's that," she said.

"That what?"

"That!" she said unwavering.

"That?"

We would have been stuck indefinitely in a round of "that?" and "that!" if not for the exceptional will of that child, who, without a word, solely through the extreme authority of her stare, compelled me to hear what she herself was hearing. In the rapt silence she had forced on me, I finally heard the faint peeping of the chick in the kitchen.

"It's the chick."

"Chick?" she said, extremely suspicious.

"I bought a chick," I replied in resignation.

"A chick!" she repeated as if I'd insulted her.

"A chick."

And we would have been stuck there. If not for a certain something I saw and that I'd never seen before.

What was it? But, whatever it was, it was no longer there. A chick had twinkled for a second in her eyes and submerged into them never to have existed. And the shadow had fallen. A deep shadow across the land. From the instant her trembling mouth had been on the verge of involuntarily thinking "I want one too," from that instant the darkness had gathered in the depths of her eyes in a retractable desire that, if anyone touched her, would shut even tighter like the leaves of a bashful mimosa. And would shrink before the impossible, the impossible that came close and, in temptation, had almost been hers: the darkness in her eyes flickered like a gold coin. A certain mischief then passed over her face — if I hadn't been there, out of mischief, she'd have stolen anything. In those eyes blinking with dissimulated wisdom, in her eyes that great propensity for plunder. She glanced at me, and it was envy, you have everything, and reproach, since we're not the same and I have a chick, and covetousness — she wanted me for herself. Slowly I started leaning into the back of my chair, her envy that bared my poverty, and turned my poverty pensive; if I hadn't been there, she'd have stolen my poverty too; she wanted everything. After the covetous tremor faded, the darkness in her eyes suffered in full: I hadn't just exposed her to an unsheltered face, I had now exposed her to the best thing in the world: a chick. Without seeing me, her hot eyes stared at me in an intense abstraction that placed itself in intimate contact with my intimate self. Something was happening that I couldn't manage to understand with the naked eye. And once more the desire came back. This time her eyes grew anguished as if there was nothing they could do with the rest of her body that was independently pulling away. And they grew even wider, alarmed at the physical force of the decomposition happening inside her. Her delicate mouth became a little childish, a bruised purple. She looked at the ceiling—the circles under her eyes gave her an air of supreme martyrdom. Without moving, I was looking at her. I knew about the high incidence of infant mortality. In her case I got swept up in the great question: is it worthwhile? I don't know, my increasing stillness told her, but that's how it is. There, faced with my silence, she was giving herself over to the process, and if she asked me the great question, it would have to go unanswered. She had to give herself—for nothing. That's how it would have to be. And for nothing. She was clinging to something inside herself, not wanting it. But I was waiting. I knew that we are the thing that must happen. I could only help her in silence. And, dazzled by misunderstanding, I heard a heart beating inside me that wasn't mine. Before my fascinated eyes, right there before me, like an ectoplasm, she was being transformed into a child.

Not without pain. In silence I was seeing the pain of her difficult joy. The slow fury of a snail. She ran her tongue slowly over her thin lips. (Help me, said her body in its arduous bifurcation. I'm helping, my immobility answered.) The slow agony. She was swelling all over, slowly being deformed. There were moments her eyes became all lashes, with the eagerness of an egg. And her mouth had a trembling hunger. She was nearly smiling then, as if laid out on an operating table saying it didn't hurt that badly. She didn't lose sight of me: there were the footprints she didn't see, someone had already walked through there, and she guessed that I had walked a lot. More and more she was being deformed, nearly identical to herself. Do I risk it? do I let myself feel?, she was asking inside herself. Yes, she answered herself through me.

And my first yes intoxicated me. Yes, my silence repeated to hers, yes. As when my son was born I said to him: yes. I had the audacity to say yes to Ofélia, I who knew that we can also die in childhood without anyone noticing. Yes, I repeated intoxicated, because there is no greater danger: when you go, you go together, you yourself will always be there: that, that is what you will take along into whatever you shall be.

The agony of her birth. Until then I had never seen courage. The courage to be something other than what one is, to give birth to oneself, and to leave one's former body on the ground. And without having answered to anyone about whether it was worthwhile. "I," her fluid-soaked body was trying to say. Her nuptials with herself.

Ofélia asked slowly, wary of what was happening to her:

"Is it a chick?"

I didn't look at her.

"Yes, it's a chick."

From the kitchen came the faint peeping. We sat in silence as if Jesus had been born. Ofélia was breathing, breathing.

"A little chick?" she confirmed doubtfully.

"Yes, a little chick," I said guiding her carefully toward life.

"Oh, a little chick," she said, considering it.

"A little chick," I said without being hard on her.

For several minutes now I had found myself facing a child. The metamorphosis had occurred.

"It's in the kitchen."

"In the kitchen?" she repeated pretending not to understand.

"In the kitchen," I repeated authoritatively for the first time, without adding anything else.

"Oh, in the kitchen," Ofélia said in a very fake voice and looked up at the ceiling.

But she was suffering. Somewhat ashamed I finally realized that I was taking my revenge. She was suffering, pretending, looking at the ceiling. That mouth, those circles under her eyes.

"You can go in the kitchen and play with the chick."

"Me … ?" she asked, playing dumb.

"But only if you want to."

I know I should have ordered her to, so as to avoid exposing her to the humiliation of wanting to so badly. I know I shouldn't have given her the choice, and then she'd have the excuse of being forced to obey. But right then it wasn't out of revenge that I was giving her the torment of freedom. It was because that step, that step too she had to take on her own. On her own and now. She herself would have to go to the mountain. Why—I was confusing myself—why am I trying to breathe my life into her purple mouth? why am I giving her breath? how dare I breathe into her, if I myself … —just so she can walk, I am giving her these arduous steps? I breathe my life into her just so that one day, exhausted, she for an instant can feel that the mountain went to her?

It would be my right. But I had no choice. It was an emergency as if the girl's lips were turning more and more purple.

"Only go see the little chick if you want to," I then repeated with the extreme severity of someone saving another.

We sat face to face, dissimilar, bodies separate from each other; only hostility united us. I was harsh and inert in my chair so that the girl would cause herself pain inside another being, firm so she would struggle inside of me; getting stronger the more that Ofélia needed to hate me and needed me to resist the suffering of her hatred. I cannot live this for you—my coldness said to her. Her struggle was happening ever closer and inside me, as if that individual who at birth had been extraordinarily endowed with strength were drinking of my weakness. By using me she was hurting me with her strength; she was clawing at me while trying to cling to my smooth walls. Finally her voice resounded in soft and slow anger:

"I guess I'll go see the chick in the kitchen."

"Go ahead," I said slowly.

She took her time, trying to maintain the dignity in her back.

She came back from the kitchen immediately—she was amazed, unabashed, showing the chick in her hand, and with a bewilderment in her eyes that wholly questioned me:

"It's a little chick!" she said.

She looked at it in her outstretched hand, looked at me, then looked back at her hand—and suddenly filled with an anxiousness and worry that automatically drew me into anxiousness and worry.

"But it's a little chick!" she said, and reproach immediately flickered in her eyes as if I hadn't told her who was peeping.

I laughed. Ofélia looked at me, outraged. And suddenly—

suddenly she laughed. We both burst into laughter then, a bit shrill.

After we'd laughed, Ofélia put the chick on the floor to let it walk around. If it ran, she ran after it, she seemed to let it be autonomous just so she could miss it; but if it cowered, she'd rush to protect it, sorry that it was under her control, "poor thing, he's mine"; and whenever she held it, her hand was crooked with care—it was love, yes, tortured love. He's really small, therefore you have to be really careful, we can't pet him because it's really dangerous; don't let them pick him up whenever they want, you can do what you like, ma'am, but corn's too big for his little open beak; because he's so fragile, poor thing, so young, therefore you can't let your sons pet him; only I know how he likes to be petted; he keeps on slipping, therefore the kitchen floor isn't the right place for a little chick.

For quite some time I'd been trying to go back to typing in an attempt to make up for all that lost time and with Ofélia lulling me, and gradually talking only to the little chick, and loving with love. For the first time she'd dropped me, she was no longer me. I looked at her, all golden as she was, and the chick all golden, and the two of them humming like distaff and spindle. And my freedom at last, and without a rupture; farewell, and I was smiling with nostalgia.

Much later I realized that Ofélia was talking to me.

"I think—I think I'm going to put him in the kitchen."

"Go ahead."

I didn't see when she left, I didn't see when she returned. At some point, by chance and distractedly, I sensed how long things had been quiet. I looked at her for an instant. She was seated, fingers clasped on her lap. Without knowing exactly why, I looked at her a second time:

"What is it?"

"Me ...?"

"Are you feeling sick?"

"Me ...?"

"Do you want to go to the bathroom?"

"Me ...?"

I gave up, went back to the typewriter. A while later I heard her voice:

"I'm going to have to go home."

"All right."

"If you let me, ma'am."

I looked at her in surprise:

"Well, if you want to ..."

"Then," she said, "then I'm going."

She left walking slowly, shut the door without a sound. I kept staring at the closed door. You're the weird one, I thought. I went back to work.

But I couldn't make it past the same sentence. Okay—I thought impatiently looking at my watch—and what is it now? I sat there interrogating myself halfheartedly, seeking within myself for what could be interrupting me. When I was about to give up, I recalled an extremely still face: Ofélia. Something not quite an idea flashed through my head which, at the unexpected thought, tilted to better hear what I was sensing. Slowly I pushed the typewriter away. Reluctant, I slowly moved the chairs out of my way. Until I paused slowly at the kitchen door. On the floor was the dead chick. Ofélia! I called in an impulse for the girl who had fled.

From an infinite distance I saw the floor. Ofélia, I tried in vain to bridge the distance to the speechless girl's heart. Oh, don't be so afraid! sometimes we kill out of love, but I swear that some day we forget, I swear! we don't love very well, listen, I repeated as if I could reach her before, giving up on serving the truth, she'd haughtily serve the nothing. I who hadn't remembered to warn her that without fear there was the world. But I swear that is what breathing is. I was very tired, I sat on the kitchen stool.

Where I am now, slowly beating the batter for tomorrow's cake. Sitting, as if for all these years I've been waiting patiently in the kitchen. Under the table, today's chick trembles. The yellow is the same, the beak is the same. As we are promised on Easter, in December he will return. Ofélia is the one who didn't return: she grew up. She went off to become the Hindu princess her tribe awaited in the desert.

Mineirinho

YES, I SUPPOSE IT IS IN MYSELF, AS ONE OF THE REP-
resentatives of us, that I should seek the reasons why the death
of a thug is hurting. And why it does me more good to count
the thirteen gunshots that killed Mineirinho rather than his
crimes. I asked my cook what she thought about it. I saw in
her face the slight convulsion of a conflict, the distress of not
understanding what one feels, of having to betray contradic-
tory feelings because one cannot reconcile them. Indisputable
facts, but indisputable revolt as well, the violent compassion
of revolt. Feeling divided by one's own confusion about being
unable to forget that Mineirinho was dangerous and had already killed too many; and still we wanted him to live. The
cook grew slightly guarded, seeing me perhaps as an aveng-
ing justice. Somewhat angry at me, who was prying into her
soul, she answered coldly: "It's no use saying what I feel. Who
doesn't know Mineirinho was a criminal? But I'm sure he was
saved and is already in heaven." I answered, "more than lots of
people who haven't killed anyone."

Why? For the first law, the one that protects the irreplace-
able body and life, is thou shalt not kill. It is my greatest as-
surance: that way they won't kill me, because I don't want to
die, and that way they won't let me kill, because having killed
would be darkness for me.

This is the law. But there is something that, if it makes me hear the first and the second gunshots with the relief of safety, at the third puts me on the alert, at the fourth unsettles me, the fifth and the sixth cover me in shame, the seventh and eighth I hear with my heart pounding in horror, at the ninth and tenth my mouth is quivering, at the eleventh I say God's name in fright, at the twelfth I call to my brother. The thirteenth shot murders me—because I am the other. Because I want to be the other.

That justice that watches over my sleep, I repudiate it, humiliated that I need it. Meanwhile I sleep and falsely save myself. We, the essential frauds. For my house to function, I demand as my primary duty that I be a fraud, that I not exercise my revolt and my love, both set aside. If I am not a fraud, my house trembles. I must have forgotten that beneath the house is the land, the ground upon which a new house might be erected. Meanwhile we sleep and falsely save ourselves. Until thirteen gunshots wake us up, and in horror I plead too late—twenty-eight years after Mineirinho was born—that in killing this cornered man, they do not kill him in us. Because I know that he is my error. And out of a whole lifetime, by God, sometimes the only thing that saves a person is error, and I know that we shall not be saved so long as our error is not precious to us. My error is my mirror, where I see what in silence I made of a man. My error is the way I saw life opening up in his flesh and I was aghast, and I saw the substance of life, placenta and blood, the living mud. In Mineirinho my way of living burst. How could I not love him, if he lived up till the thirteenth gunshot the very thing that I had been sleeping? His frightened violence. His innocent violence—not in its consequences, but innocent in itself as that of a son whose father neglected him.

Everything that was violence in him is furtive in us, and we avoid each other's gaze so as not to run the risk of understanding each other. So that the house won't tremble. The violence bursting in Mineirinho that only another man's hand, the hand of hope, resting on his stunned and wounded head, could appease and make his startled eyes lift and at last fill with tears. Only after a man is found inert on the ground, without his cap or shoes, do I see that I forgot to tell him: me too.

I don't want this house. I want a justice that would have given a chance to something pure and full of helplessness in Mineirinho—that thing that moves mountains and is the same as what made him love a woman "like a madman," and the same that led him through a doorway so narrow that it slashes into nakedness; it is a thing in us as intense and transparent as a dangerous gram of radium, that thing is a grain of life that if trampled is transformed into something threatening—into trampled love; that thing, which in Mineirinho became a knife, it is the same thing in me that makes me offer another man water, not because I have water, but because, I too, know what thirst is; and I too, who have not lost my way, have experienced perdition. Prior justice, that would not make me ashamed. It was past time for us, with or without irony, to be more divine; if we can guess what God's benevolence might be it is because we guess at benevolence in ourselves, whatever sees the man before he succumbs to the sickness of crime. I go on, nevertheless, waiting for God to be the father, when I know that one man can be father to another. And I go on living in my weak house. That house, whose protective door I lock so tightly, that house won't withstand the first gale that will send a locked door flying through the air. But it is standing, and Mineirinho lived rage on my behalf, while I was calm. He was gunned down in his disoriented strength, while a god fabricated at the last second hastily blesses my composed wrongdoing and my stupefied justice: what upholds the walls of my house is the certainty that I shall always vindicate myself, my friends won't vindicate me, but my enemies who are my accomplices, they will greet me; what upholds me is knowing that I shall always fabricate a god in the image of whatever I need in order to sleep peacefully, and that others will furtively pretend that we are all in the right and that there is nothing to be done. All this, yes, for we are the essential frauds, bastions of something. And above all trying not to understand.

Because the one who understands disrupts. There is something in us that would disrupt everything—a thing that understands. That thing that stays silent before the man without his cap or shoes, and to get them he robbed and killed; and stays silent before Saint George of gold and diamonds. That very serious thing in me grows more serious still when faced with the man felled by machine guns. Is that thing the killer inside me? No, it is the despair inside us. Like madmen, we know him, that dead man in whom the gram of radium caught fire. But only like madmen, and not frauds, do we know him. It is as a madman that I enter a life that so often has no doorway, and as a madman that I comprehend things dangerous to comprehend, and only as a madman do I feel deep love, that is confirmed when I see that the radium will radiate regardless, if not through trust, hope and love, then miserably through the sick courage of destruction. If I weren't mad, I'd be eight hundred policemen with eight hundred machine guns, and this would be my honorableness.

Until a slightly madder justice came along. One that would take into account that we all must speak for a man driven to despair because in him human speech has already failed, he is already so mute that only a brute incoherent cry serves as signal. A prior justice that would recall how our great struggle is that of fear, and that a man who kills many does so because he was very much afraid. Above all a justice that would examine itself, and see that all of us, living mud, are dark, and that is why not even one man's wrongdoing can be surrendered to another man's wrongdoing: so that this other man cannot commit, freely and with approbation, the crime of gunning someone down. A justice that does not forget that we are all dangerous, and that the moment that the deliverer of justice kills, he is no longer protecting us or trying to eliminate a criminal, he is committing his own personal crime, one long held inside him. At the moment he kills a criminal—in that instant an innocent is killed. No, it's not that I want the sublime, nor for things to turn into words to make me sleep peacefully, a combination of forgiveness, of vague charity, we who seek shelter in the abstract.

What I want is much rougher and more difficult: I want the land.

Covert Joy
("Felicidade clandestina")

SHE WAS FAT, SHORT, FRECKLED, AND HAD REDDISH, excessively frizzy hair. She had a huge bust, while the rest of us were still flat-chested. As if that weren't enough, she'd fill both pockets of her blouse, over her bust, with candy. But she had what any child devourer of stories would wish for: a father who owned a bookstore.

She didn't take much advantage of it. And we even less: even for birthdays, instead of at least a cheap little book, she'd present us with a postcard from her father's shop. Even worse, it would be a view of Recife itself, where we lived, with the bridges we'd seen countless times. On the back she'd write in elaborately curlicued script words like "birthday" and "thinking of you."

But what a talent she had for cruelty. She was pure vengeance, sucking noisily on her candy. How that girl must have hated us, we who were unforgivably pretty, slender, tall, with flowing hair. She performed her sadism on me with calm ferocity. In my eagerness to read, I didn't even notice the humiliations to which she subjected me: I kept begging her to lend me the books she wasn't reading.

Until the momentous day came for her to start performing a kind of Chinese torture on me. As if in passing, she informed me that she owned *The Shenanigans of Little Miss Snub-Nose*, by Monteiro Lobato.

It was a thick book, my God, it was a book you could live with, eating it, sleeping it. And completely beyond my means. She told me to stop by her house the next day and she'd lend it to me.

Up until the next day I was transformed into the very hope of joy itself: I wasn't living, I was swimming slowly in a gentle sea, the waves carrying me to and fro.

The next day I went to her house, literally running. She didn't live above a shop like me, but rather in a whole house. She didn't ask me in. Looking me right in the eye, she said she'd lent the book to another girl, and that I should come back the next day. Mouth agape, I left slowly, but soon enough hope completely took over again and I started back down the street skipping, which was my strange way of moving through the streets of Recife. This time I didn't even fall: the promise of the book guided me, the next day would come, the next days would later become the rest of my life, love for the world awaited me, I went skipping through the streets as usual and didn't fall once.

But things didn't simply end there. The secret plan of the bookseller's daughter was serene and diabolical. The next day, there I stood at her front door, with a smile and my heart beating. Only to hear her calm reply: the book hadn't been returned yet, and I should come back the next day. Little did I know how later on, over the course of my life, the drama of "the next day" with her would repeat itself with my heart beating.

And so it went. For how long? I don't know. She knew it

would be for an indefinite time, until the bile oozed completely out of her thick body. I had already started to guess that she'd chosen me to suffer, sometimes I guess things. But, in actually guessing things, I sometimes accept them: as if whoever wants to make me suffer damn well needs me to.

For how long? I'd go to her house daily, without missing a single day. Sometimes she'd say: well I had the book yesterday afternoon, but you didn't come till this morning, so I lent it to another girl. And I, who didn't usually get dark circles under my eyes, felt those dark circles deepening under my astonished eyes.

Until one day, when I was at her front door, listening humbly and silently to her refusal, her mother appeared. She must have been wondering about the mute, daily appearance of that girl at her front door. She asked us to explain. There was a silent commotion, interrupted by words that didn't clarify much. The lady found it increasingly strange that she wasn't understanding. Until that good mother understood. She turned to her daughter and with enormous surprise exclaimed: But that book never left the house and you didn't even want to read it!

And the worst thing for that woman wasn't realizing what was going on. It must have been the horrified realization of the kind of daughter she had. She eyed us in silence: the power of perversity in the daughter she didn't know and the little blond girl standing at the door, exhausted, out in the wind of the streets of Recife. That was when, finally regaining her composure, she said to her daughter firmly and calmly: you're going to lend that book right this minute. And to me: "And you can keep that book for as long as you like." Do you understand? It was worth more than giving me the book: "for as long as I liked" is all that a person, big or small, could ever dare wish for.

How can I explain what happened next? I was stunned, and just like that the book was in my hand. I don't think I said a thing. I took the book. No, I didn't go skipping off as usual. I walked away very slowly. I know that I was holding the thick book with both hands, clutching it against my chest. As for how long it took to get home, that doesn't really matter either. My chest was hot, my heart thoughtful.

When I got home, I didn't start reading. I pretended not to have it, just so later on I could feel the shock of having it. Hours later I opened it, read a few wondrous lines, closed it again, wandered around the house, stalled even more by eating some bread and butter, pretended not to know where I had put the book, found it, opened it for a few seconds. I kept inventing the most contrived obstacles for that covert thing that was joy. Joy would always be covert for me. I must have already sensed it. Oh how I took my time! I was living in the clouds ... There was pride and shame inside me. I was a delicate queen.

Sometimes I'd sit in the hammock, swinging with the book open on my lap, not touching it, in the purest ecstasy.

I was no longer a girl with a book: I was a woman with her lover.

Remnants of Carnival
("Restos do Carnaval")

NO, NOT THIS PAST CARNIVAL. BUT I DON'T KNOW why this one transported me back to my childhood and those Ash Wednesdays on the dead streets where the remains of streamers and confetti fluttered. The occasional devout woman with a veil covering her head would be heading to church, crossing the street left so incredibly empty after Carnival. Until the next year. And when the celebration was fast approaching, what could explain the inner tumult that came over me? As if the budding world were finally opening into a big scarlet rose. As if the streets and squares of Recife were finally explaining why they'd been made. As if human voices were finally singing the capacity for pleasure that was kept secret in me. Carnival was mine, mine.

However, in reality, I barely participated at all. I had never been to a children's ball, they'd never dressed me up in costume. To make up for it, they'd let me stay up until eleven in the front stairwell of the house where we lived, eagerly watching others have fun. I'd get two precious things that I saved up greedily so they'd last all three days: some party spray and a bag of confetti. Ah, it's getting hard to write. Because I'm feeling how my heart is going to darken as I realize how, even barely joining in the merriment, my yearning was such that even next to nothing made me a happy little girl.

And the masks? I was afraid but it was a vital and necessary fear for it went along with my deepest suspicion that the human face was also a kind of mask. In my front stairwell, if someone in a mask spoke to me, I'd suddenly come into indispensable contact with my inner world, which was made not only of elves and enchanted princes, but of people with their mystery. Even my fright at the people in masks, then, was essential for me.

They didn't dress me up: with all the worry about my sick mother, no one at home could spare a thought for a child's Carnival. But I'd ask one of my sisters to curl that straight hair of mine that I so hated and then I'd take pride in having wavy hair for at least three days a year. During those three days, moreover, my sister gave in to my intense dream of being a young lady—I could hardly wait to leave behind a vulnerable childhood—and she painted my lips with bright lipstick, putting rouge on my cheeks too. Then I felt pretty and feminine, I was no longer a kid.

But there was one Carnival that was different from the rest. So miraculous that I couldn't quite believe so much had been granted me, I, who had long since learned to ask for little. What happened was that a friend's mother had decided to dress up her daughter and the costume pattern was named the *Rose*. To make it she bought sheets and sheets of pink crepe paper, from which, I suppose, she planned to imitate the petals of a flower. Mouth agape, I watched the costume gradually taking shape and being created. Though the crepe paper didn't remotely resemble petals, I solemnly believed it was one of the most beautiful costumes I had ever seen.

That's when simply by chance the unexpected happened: there was leftover crepe paper, and quite a bit. And my friend's mother—perhaps heeding my mute appeal, the mute despair of my envy, or perhaps out of sheer kindness, since there was leftover paper—decided to make me a *rose* costume too with the remaining materials. So for that Carnival, for the first time in my life I would get what I had always wanted: I would be something other than myself.

Even the preparations left me dizzy with joy. I had never felt so busy: down to the last detail, my friend and I planned everything out, we'd wear slips under our costumes, so if it rained and the costume melted away at least we'd still be somewhat dressed—the very idea of a sudden downpour that would leave us, in our eight-year-old feminine modesty, wearing slips on the street, made us die of anticipated shame—but oh! God would help us! it wouldn't rain! As for the fact that my costume existed solely thanks to the other girl's leftovers, I swallowed, with some pain, my pride, which had always been fierce, and I humbly accepted the handout destiny was offering me.

But why did precisely that Carnival, the only one in costume, have to be so melancholy? Early Sunday morning I already had my hair in curlers, so the waves would hold longer. But the minutes weren't passing, because I was so anxious. Finally, finally! three in the afternoon arrived: careful not to tear the paper, I dressed up as a *rose*.

Many things much worse than these have happened to me, that I've forgiven. Yet I still can't even understand this one now: is a toss of the dice for a *destiny* irrational? It's merciless. When I was all dressed in the crepe paper and ready, with my hair still in curlers and not yet wearing lipstick or rouge—my mother's health suddenly took a turn for the worse, an abrupt upheaval broke out at home, and they sent me quickly to buy medicine at the pharmacy. I ran off dressed as a *rose*—but my still-bare face wasn't wearing the young-lady mask that would have covered my utterly exposed childish life—I ran and ran, bewildered, alarmed, amid streamers, confetti and shouts of Carnival. Other people's merriment stunned me.

When hours later the atmosphere at home calmed down, my sister did my hair and makeup. But something had died inside me. And, as in the stories I'd read about fairies who were always casting and breaking spells, the spell on me had been broken; I was no longer a *rose*, I was once again just a little girl. I went out to the street and standing there I wasn't a flower, I was a brooding clown with scarlet lips. In my hunger to feel ecstasy, I'd sometimes started to cheer up but in remorse I'd recall my mother's grave condition and once again I'd die.

Only hours later did salvation come. And if I quickly clung to it, that's because I so badly needed to be saved. A boy of twelve or so, which for me meant a young man, this very handsome boy stopped before me and, in a combination of tenderness, crudeness, playfulness and sensuality, he covered my hair, straight by now, with confetti: for an instant we stood face to face, smiling, without speaking. And then I, a little woman of eight, felt for the rest of the night that someone had finally recognized me: I was, indeed, a rose.

The Waters of the World
("As águas do mundo")

THERE IT IS, THE SEA, THE MOST UNINTELLIGIBLE OF non-human existences. And here is the woman, standing on the beach, the most unintelligible of living beings. As a human being she once posed a question about herself, becoming the most unintelligible of living beings. She and the sea.

Their mysteries could only meet if one surrendered to the other: the surrender of two unknowable worlds made with the trust by which two understandings would surrender to each other.

She looks at the sea, that's what she can do. It is only cut off for her by the line of the horizon, that is, by her human incapacity to see the Earth's curvature.

It is six in the morning. There is only a free dog hesitating on the beach, a black dog. Why is a dog so free? Because it is the living mystery that doesn't wonder about itself. The woman hesitates because she's about to go in.

Her body soothes itself with its own slightness compared to the vastness of the sea because it's her body's slightness that lets her stay warm and it's this slightness that makes her a poor and free person, with her portion of a dog's freedom on the sands. That body will enter the limitless cold that roars without rage in the silence of six o'clock. The woman doesn't know it: but she's fulfilling a courage. With the beach empty at this morning hour, she doesn't have the example of other humans who transform the entry into the sea into a simple lighthearted game of living. She is alone. The salty sea is not alone because it's salty and vast, and this is an achievement. Right then she knows herself even less than she knows the sea. Her courage comes from not knowing herself, but going ahead nevertheless. Not knowing yourself is inevitable, and not knowing yourself demands courage.

She goes in. The salt water is cold enough to make her legs shiver in a ritual. But an inevitable joy—joy is an inevitability—has already seized her, though smiling doesn't even occur to her. On the contrary, she is very serious. The smell is of a heady sea air that awakens her most dormant age-old slumbers. And now she is alert, even without thinking, as a hunter is alert without thinking. The woman is now a compact and a light and a sharp one—and cuts a path through the iciness that, liquid, opposes her, yet lets her in, as in love when opposition can be a request.

The slow journey fortifies her secret courage. And suddenly she lets herself be covered by the first wave. The salt, iodine, everything liquid, blind her for a few instants, streaming all over—surprised standing up, fertilized.

Now the cold becomes frigid. Moving ahead, she splits the sea down the middle. She no longer needs courage, now already ancient in the ritual. She lowers her head into the shine of the sea, and then lifts out the hair that emerges streaming over her salty eyes that are stinging. She plays with her hand in the water, leisurely, her hair in the sun almost immediately stiffens with salt. With cupped hands she does what she's always done in the sea, and with the pride of people who never explain even to themselves: with cupped hands filled with water, she drinks in great, good gulps.

And that was what she'd been missing: the sea inside her like the thick liquid of a man. Now she's entirely equal to herself. Her nourished throat constricts from the salt, her eyes redden from the salt dried by the sun, the gentle waves slap against her and retreat for she is a compact embankment.

She dives again, again drinks more water, no longer greedy for she doesn't need more. She is the lover who knows she'll have everything all over again. The sun rises higher and makes her bristle as it dries her, she dives again: she is ever less greedy and less sharp. Now she knows what she wants. She wants to stand still inside the sea. So she does. As against the sides of a ship, the water slaps, retreats, slaps. The woman receives no transmissions. She doesn't need communication.

Afterward she walks in the water back to the beach. She's not walking on the water—ah she'd never do that since they walked on water millennia ago—but no one can keep her from: walking in the water. Sometimes the sea resists her, powerfully dragging her backward, but then the woman's prow pushes ahead a bit harder and tougher.

And now she steps onto the sand. She knows she is glistening with water, and salt and sun. Even if she forgets a few minutes from now, she can never lose all this. And she knows in some obscure way that her streaming hair is that of a castaway. Because she knows—she knows she has created a danger. A danger as ancient as the human being.

He Drank Me Up
("Ele me bebeu")

YES. IT ACTUALLY HAPPENED.

Serjoca was a makeup artist. But he didn't want anything to do with women. He wanted men.

And he always did Aurélia Nascimento's makeup. Aurélia was pretty and, with makeup on, she was a knockout. She was blonde, wore a wig and false eyelashes. They became friends. They went out together, the kind of thing where you go out to dinner at a nightclub.

Whenever Aurélia wanted to look beautiful she called Serjoca. Serjoca was good-looking too. He was slim and tall.

And that's how things went. A phone call and they'd make a date. She'd get dressed up, she went all out. She wore contact lenses. And stuffed her bra. But her own breasts were beautiful, pointy. She only stuffed her bra because she was flat-chested. Her mouth was a rosy red bud. And her teeth large and white.

One day, at six in the evening, at the peak of rush hour, Aurélia and Serjoca were standing outside the Copacabana Palace Hotel and waiting in vain for a taxi. Serjoca, worn out, was leaning against a tree. Aurélia impatient. She suggested giving the doorman ten cruzeiros to hail them a taxi. Serjoca refused: he was cheap.

It was almost seven. Getting dark. What to do?

Nearby was Affonso Carvalho. Metals magnate. He was waiting for his Mercedes and chauffeur. It was hot, the car was air-conditioned, with a phone and a fridge. Affonso had turned forty the day before.

He saw Aurélia's impatience as she tapped her feet on the sidewalk. An attractive woman, thought Affonso. And in need of a ride. He turned to her:

"Having trouble finding a cab, miss?"

"I've been here since six o'clock and not one taxi has stopped to pick us up! I can't take it anymore."

"My chauffeur's coming soon," Affonso said. "Can I give you a lift somewhere?"

"I'd be so grateful, especially since my feet are hurting."

But she didn't say she had corns. She hid her flaw. She was heavily made-up and looked at the man with desire. Serjoca very quiet.

Finally the chauffeur pulled up, got out, opened the door. The three of them got in. She in front, next to the chauffeur, the two of them in the backseat. She took off her shoes discreetly and sighed in relief.

"Where do you want to go?"

"We don't exactly have a destination," Aurélia said, increasingly turned on by Affonso's manly face.

He said:

"What if we went to Number One for a drink?"

"I'd love to," Aurélia said. "Wouldn't you, Serjoca?"

"Sure. I could use a stiff drink."

So they went to the club, at this nearly deserted hour. And chatted. Affonso talked about metallurgy. The other two didn't understand a thing. But they pretended to. It was tedious. But Affonso got all worked up and, under the table, slid his foot against Aurélia's. The very foot that had corns. She reciprocated, aroused. Then Affonso said:

"What if we went back to my place for dinner? Today I've got escargot and chicken with truffles. How about it?"

"I'm famished."

And Serjoca silent. Affonso turned him on too.

The apartment was carpeted in white and there was a Bruno Giorgi sculpture. They sat down, had another drink and went into the dining room. A jacaranda table. A waiter serving from the left. Serjoca didn't know how to eat escargot and got all tripped up by the special utensils. He didn't like it. But Aurélia really liked it, though she was afraid of getting garlic breath. But they drank French champagne all through dinner. No one wanted dessert, all they wanted was coffee.

And they went into the living room. Then Serjoca came to life. And started talking nonstop. He cast bedroom eyes at the industrialist. Affonso was astounded by the handsome young man's eloquence. The next day he'd call Aurélia to tell her: Serjoca is the most charming person.

And they made another date. This time at a restaurant, the Albamar. To start, they had oysters. Once again, Serjoca had a hard time eating the oysters. I'm a loser, he thought.

But before they all met up, Aurélia had called Serjoca: she urgently needed her makeup done. He went over to her place.

Then, while she was getting her makeup done, she thought: Serjoca's taking off my face.

She got the feeling he was erasing her features: empty, a face made only of flesh. Dark flesh.

She felt distress. She excused herself and went to the bathroom to look at herself in the mirror. It was just as she'd imagined: Serjoca had annulled her face. Even her bones—and she had spectacular bone structure—even her bones had disappeared. He's drinking me up, she thought, he's going to destroy me. And all because of Affonso.

She returned out of sorts. At the restaurant she hardly spoke. Affonso talked more with Serjoca, barely glancing at Aurélia: he was interested in the young man.

Finally, finally lunch was over.

Serjoca made a date with Affonso for that evening. Aurélia said she couldn't make it, she was tired. It was a lie: she wasn't going because she had no face to show.

She got home, took a long bubble bath, lay there thinking: before you know it he'll take away my body too. What could she do to take back what had been hers? Her individuality?

She got out of the bathtub lost in thought. She dried off with a huge red towel. Lost in thought the whole time. She stepped onto the scale: she was at a good weight. Before you know it he'll take away my weight too, she thought.

She went over to the mirror. She looked at herself deeply. But she was no longer anything.

Then—then all of a sudden she slapped herself brutally on the left side of her face. To wake herself up. She stood still looking at herself. And, as if that weren't enough, she slapped her face twice more. To find herself.

And it really happened.

In the mirror she finally saw a human face, sad, delicate. She was Aurélia Nascimento. She had just been born. Nas-ci-men-to.*

---

* "Birth."

That's Where I'm Going
("É para lá que eu vou")

BEYOND THE EAR THERE IS A SOUND, AT THE FAR END of sight a view, at the tips of the fingers an object—that's where I'm going.

At the tip of the pencil the line.

Where a thought expires is an idea, at the final breath of joy another joy, at the point of the sword magic—that's where I'm going.

At the tips of the toes the leap.

It's like the story of someone who went and didn't return—that's where I'm going.

Or am I? Yes, I'm going. And I'll return to see how things are. Whether they're still magic. Reality? I await you all. That's where I'm going.

At the tip of the word is the word. I want to use the word "soirée" and don't know where and when. At the edge of the soirée is the family. At the edge of the family am I. At the edge of I is me. To me is where I'm going. And from me I go out to see. See what? to see what exists. After I am dead to reality is where I'm going. For now it is a dream. A fateful dream. But later—later all is real. And the free soul seeks a place to settle into. Me is an I that I proclaim. I don't know what I'm talking about. I'm talking about the nothing. I am nothing. Once dead I shall expand and disperse, and someone will say my name with love.

To my poor name is where I'm going.

And from there I'll return to call the names of my beloved and my sons. They will answer me. At last I shall have an answer. What answer? that of love. Love: I love you all so much. I love love. Love is red. Jealousy is green. My eyes are green. But they're so dark a green that in photographs they look black. My secret is having green eyes and nobody knows it.

At the far end of me is I. I, imploring, I the one who needs, who begs, who cries, who laments. Yet who sings. Who speaks words. Words on the wind? who cares, the winds bring them back and I possess them.

I at the edge of the wind. The wuthering heights call to me. I go, witch that I am. And I am transmuted.

Oh, dog, where is your soul? is it at the edge of your body? I am at the edge of my body. And I waste away slowly.

What am I saying? I am saying love. And at the edge of love are we.

Keeper of the Egg: an afterword

THE AWKWARD CHICKEN. THE SURE EGG. THE FRIGHT-
ened chicken. The sure egg.

*The egg is the chicken's unattainable dream. The chicken loves
the egg.* Clarice Lispector's words flit around my brain as I
grasp them gently, just enough to carry them into a new language, trying not to understand too completely. *Understanding
is the proof of error. The chicken's inner life consists of acting as if
she understands.*

We are the chicken and Clarice, the egg. The egg is the ideal
form that transcends time and can never be other than itself
(*You are perfect, egg*). The chicken is never quite sure how to
proceed, stuck in the present and continually trying to figure
herself out. I know it is wrong to read her most elusive story,
"The Egg and the Chicken," so schematically, especially when
it is a meditation on the impossibility of truly perceiving and
conceiving a thing (the egg). Clarice called the story "a mystery
to me" and would put herself on the side of the chicken. But
I can't help thinking of this relationship of translator to au-
thor, or translation to original, in these terms: the chicken as

unlikely keeper of the egg. *The chicken exists so that the egg can traverse the ages.* I picture the little beating heart of the tragicomic heroine of "A Chicken," who saves herself from immediate doom by laying an astonishing egg.

Over a decade has passed since I first began translating Lispector's *Complete Stories*. The writer who was famous in Brazil yet remained a cult figure abroad has gained a worldwide following among new generations of readers and no longer needs to be introduced as the Brazilian Virginia Woolf, a female Kafka, or Chekhov on the beach. I used to claim total recall of the decisions that shaped every sentence in that 2015 collection of eighty-six stories spanning Clarice Lispector's writing life, from the first story she published, at nineteen, in 1940, to the stories left on her desk when she died in 1977. That acute connection has faded, yet even casually flipping through these twenty stories, I've felt wave after wave of volatile energy crash out: the dual intensities of the stories themselves and of the two years I spent inhabiting them. I feared falling back into Clarice's marvelous abyss, the way Ana in "Love" resists the unsettling intoxication of the botanical garden, "a world to sink one's teeth into, a world of voluminous dahlias and tulips."

And I worried about second-guessing past decisions. Stumbling over choices that now felt odd, I had to recall how subtly disorienting her language is, with its slightly foreign-sounding syntax and the either too few or too many commas that disrupt the pace of reading. As I accompanied Laura's excruciating habit of overthinking every move to the point of paralysis in "The Imitation of the Rose," my heart constricted with self-recognition. While working on that story, I'd gone around and around in mental eddies, wavering over details like how to capture the hair's-breadth distinction between *ponta* and *ponto* in "that tiniest point (*ponta*) of surprise lodged in the depths of her eyes, in that tiniest offended speck (*ponto*)…"

Yet the overwhelming feeling that arises when I revisit these stories is pleasure, sometimes of a painful variety, as when strong emotions or sharply apprehended truths make us tear up, but more often in surges of joy, as Clarice's characters often experience. Her writing continues to surprise and delight me with its comic precision and moving tenderness, the breathtaking lushness of its lyricism, and its daring swerves in tone and style that intrude on her literary and philosophical modes with some wacky or incongruous element: a werewolf, the Planet Mars, a product placement for Coca-Cola. And there's the thrill of a Claricean turn of phrase that rearranges everyday experience into strange, newly reverberating shapes, as when she describes a woman riding a rollercoaster—"the triumphant fury with which her seat hurtled her into the nothing"—or a moment of stark revelation—"She was facing the oyster." (!!!)

Most of the stories in this unique edition come from Clarice Lispector's two most famous collections, *Family Ties* (1960) and *The Foreign Legion* (1964), which mark the period considered her golden era, when critical acclaim converged with popular success, after she'd struggled to publish her books during the prior decade. It also coincided with her 1959 return to Rio de Janeiro after leaving her diplomat husband, Maury Gurgel Valente. They had married in 1943—the year she published her acclaimed debut novel, *Near To the Wild Heart*—and lived in Europe and Washington D.C. for most of their time together.

The first eight of these *selected stories*, from "Love" to "The Buffalo," comprise over half of *Family Ties*, a bestseller that won Brazil's top literary prize. The writer Erico Verissimo called it "the most important story collection published in this country since Machado de Assis," and one critic hailed Clarice as "one of the best Brazilian writers of all time." She wrote the two earliest stories included here, "Mystery in São Cristóvão" and "Family Ties," in Bern, Switzerland, in 1948, the year her first son, Pedro, was born. Her younger son, Paulo, was born in D.C. in 1953, two years before she completed the stories in *Family Ties*. The most significant change that I've undergone since translating Clarice is becoming a mother, and in rereading these stories, I have been struck with unexpected force by her depictions of motherhood: both its relentless physical exertion and its spiritual tug-of-war, pitting an elemental need to nourish and protect against the urge to recover one's solitary self.

The next seven selections, from "Monkeys" to "Mineirinho," come from *The Foreign Legion*, much of which was published in magazines and newspapers in the 1960s, though the earliest, "Journey to Petrópolis," first appeared in 1949. It also includes the two stories that Clarice singled out as her favorites: "The Egg and the Chicken" and "Mineirinho," a *crônica* first published in *Senhor* magazine as a cry of revolt against the notorious May 1962 police shooting of an escaped convict in Rio.

The last five stories feature in collections published during Clarice's final decade. The classics "Covert Joy" and "Remnants of Carnival" conjure her childhood in Brazil's northeastern city of Recife and appeared in *Covert Joy* (1971) alongside the hypnotic reverie, "The Waters of the World." "He Drank Me Up" offers a taste of the campy, anarchic spirit of Clarice's late style, when she dwelled on themes of bodily desire and mortality. It is one of thirteen stories in *The Via Crucis of the Body*, which she wrote in one weekend in May 1974 and prefaced with the declaration, "Someone read my stories and said that's not literature, it's trash. I agree. But there's a time for everything.

There's also the time for trash." The final story, "That's Where I'm Going," comes from her April 1974 collection, *Where Were You at Night*. To me, it is the closest thing to a prose poem that Clarice wrote, and a fitting farewell.

In it, she leaves us, as always, with a question—*What am I saying?*—and at the edge of love.

KATRINA DODSON